Infected Be the Air

Infected Be the Air

Janice Law

Walker and Company
New York

FIC

First published in the United States of America in 1991
by Walker Publishing Company, Inc.

Published simultaneously in Canada by Thomas Allen & Son
Canada, Limited, Markham, Ontario

Library of Congress Cataloging-in-Publication Data
Law, Janice.
Infected be the air / Janice Law.
p.   cm.
ISBN 0-8027-5799-5
I. Title.
PS3562.A86I54   1991
813'.54—dc20   91-3466
CIP

Printed in the United States of America
2 4 6 8 10 9 7 5 3 1

Infected be the air whereon they ride;
And damn'd all those that trust them.

—*Macbeth*, IV.i.138

$\triangledown$

1

AT THE AGE WHEN my friends were going to law school or getting their real estate licenses, I took up organic gardening with a women's commune in northeastern Connecticut. It's none of your business why I did, and we don't need to discuss communes or the advisability of ideological communities, either. Let me just say that ours was not a success. The summer sisters decamped before the barn roof was closed in. The north pasture was rented out to a chap who runs a riding stable, and Moira and I settled in alone for the duration, supported by Nubian goats, bees, organic vegetables, and herbs.

We got along quite nicely. The new yuppie restaurants couldn't get enough of the organic, the herb-drenched, the natural, and Moira and I provided. My two kids, Doug and Julie, entered the local schools, and Moira's boy came along with his stepsister for the summers. I had no complaints, until one April afternoon when I returned from the class I teach at the U Branch to find a message from Herb Rosen. "There's some trouble with your ex," Moira said.

"Herb called? About what?"

Moira shrugged. She'd killed an elderly chicken and was energetically gutting it over a bucket in the kitchen sink.

The poultry is her department: I'm live-and-let-live where chickens are concerned. "He said urgent. That's all."

I dropped books and papers on the table and dialed. Down the line, I could hear Herb Rosen's phone ringing in the elegant teak and leather office where Max and I had settled up fifteen years of marriage with minimal interference.

"Boston, Rosen, and Hartwick."

I gave my name, but although I was told to wait, Herb came on the line almost immediately.

"Where are you, Alice?"

"I'm in the kitchen."

"I mean, you're at home? Are the kids there?"

"The kids are in school. What's this about, Herb?"

"You'd better sit down. Listen, I didn't want to be the one, but it will be on the news."

"What, Herb?" But I already knew it was bad. Car accident? Plane? Had Max been flying somewhere?

"Max is dead, Alice. They found him this morning, early. They called me. I had to identify."

"What happened to Max?" I could feel, rather than hear, my voice rising. Max was dead; I'd have to tell the children.

"He was shot."

"Murdered?"

There was silence at the other end. I could hear Herb take a deep breath. Herb, a man I'd never liked, a man who had complicated my life and tried to cut back on the divorce settlement, was on the verge of tears. "He killed himself. And he shot Bev and her boy. It was up at the cabin—maybe a week ago. But they only found them today. I had to go identify—"

I had a sudden vision of Bev, young and svelte, in a striped top and white pants, her handsome little boy holding her hand, then I said, "Max would never shoot anyone. We never had guns in the house." But I remembered the old rifle at the cabin. For vermin, for the occasional distemper-sickened fox or rabid raccoon.

"They were all there, Alice. Close range. The gun was even there. Some semiautomatic sporting thing. Listen, I can't tell you how sorry I am. Past is past. I loved that guy. Brain tumor, maybe. Stress. How the hell is anybody to know?"

I sat down at the table. "No," I said. But even then, right then, I was thinking, it had to be murder.

As Herb had predicted, the story made the evening news. We sat stunned before the tube, reluctant witnesses to disaster. We'd picked up the kids at school—Julie from the senior high building, Doug from the junior high next door. Moira had driven recklessly, which, for once, was reassuring: nothing could touch us now, not even the hairpin bend near the old quarry. When they brought Julie down to the office, I caught a glimpse of her through the glass doors: a good-looking blonde, neither child nor woman, with a sullen, vaguely nervous expression. My baby: a semi-stranger. Julie had taken the divorce hard, had blamed me. Things had come apart for her at precisely the wrong time, and the delightful little girl had grown into a wary, foulmouthed adolescent who liked older boys, ear-splitting music, and an overweight palomino that was, to my mind, her only wholesome enthusiasm.

Our eyes met as the doors opened, and I saw that some warning had already broken the exaggerated adolescent cool that was her chief weapon. "Mom, what's wrong?" she asked. "What's happened?" She looked twelve again, our last good year, and I put my arms around her and said, "Your daddy's been killed."

Ten minutes later, she was crying in the car, and I was telling Doug that he'd have to be brave, that it would be on TV, that people would be curious, maybe unkind. His face was closed, blank. He was secretive child who kept everything inside, unlike his sister, who acted things out. When we got home, I fed them strong coffee, slices of cold pizza, ice cream. On the screen, there were police cars and the flattening and distortion of familiar places. "There's the church and Peter's house," Doug said. No one answered.

The cabin seemed smaller, foreign somehow, and the familiar details—the well, the tire swing at the side, the rampant hollyhocks—only emphasized its strangeness. We were in unknown territory, all of us, where a man we'd known all our lives had murdered his girlfriend and her child, set fire to their bed, then turned the weapon on himself. We could see a blackened area above the side window, and the damaged roof, saved by a thunderstorm. The cabin might be salvageable, though with the unseasonable heat the police had had to use fans to air the place, and at this detail, Julie got up and ran into the bathroom. Doug sat staring toward the window where the evening was gathering in sheets of pink and gold. Max had done this, his father, my ex-husband, the man I'd loved.

"It appears at this time to have been a case of murder-suicide," said the announcer. He leaned self-importantly toward the camera, his microphone a baton of authority. The breeze from the lake blew his hair across his forehead, and his voice was resonant, serious, a little smug. Who was he to say? To say what appeared? Appeared was nothing. Only what is. Or was. Though "there is no art to find the mind's construction in the face," Max had never been a killer. Not for all his faults. Not ever. "I don't believe it," I said aloud. "I can't believe Max killed them."

The funeral was two weeks later, after the autopsies, the inquest, the brutal media barrage. It was a sad, noncommittal business without the noble stoicism of the Old Testament, nor the poignant hopefulness of the New. The suburban mortuary was subdued, dimly lit, a tasteful expanse of beige and dusty rose with organ music on its breath. Max's mother was too ill to travel, but his father was there, erect, dignified, white-haired, looking like the ghost of what Max should have been, would have been, in maybe thirty years: a charming old roué who'd outlived his follies and tamed his demons. I'd always liked Paul, and I hated to see his trembling step and gray cheeks. I took his hand a moment, asked after his wife, promised to bring the children out to Pittsburgh for the holidays.

"Do you believe this?" he asked.

"I'll never believe this."

He pressed my shoulder. "Max should have stayed with you," he said. Then he turned to speak to Leonard Warren, the poli-sci department chairman at the University, one of the few academics to show up. To be honest, one of the few to show up. I remembered bitterly all Max's friends and acquaintances, but that was before scandal, violence, and television news. For the children's sake, I was even glad to see Herb Rosen standing near the grave at the cemetery. He kissed me on both cheeks, hugged Julie and shook Doug's hand, then stood beside us while the carefully sealed casket was lowered into the earth. Max would have preferred cremation, but it was held to be inadvisable under the circumstances. He was a piece of forensic evidence now, liable to recall by the state. Across the grave, his father looked like chalk. A drink, I thought. I'd better see he gets home and gets a drink.

"I've got to take care of Max's dad," I said quietly to Herb.

"A moment, Alice. Let me walk you to the car. Doug and Julie can help their grandfather."

I nodded to them and turned to see what Herb was up to. He and Max had been best friends and college roommates, two of the handsomest men on campus: both clever, both charming. Max had become a professor, a philanderer, an idealist; Herb, a lawyer, the uxorious father of seven, a rich man. Now age was beginning to settle his weight around his hips, and the luxury of his dress and appointments—the Swiss watch, the cashmere jacket, the handmade shoes, the gold cuff links and tie clasp and bracelet and rings—suggested an apprentice pasha, handsome in a dark and vaguely decadent Middle-Eastern manner. His car was black, sleek, and immensely long next to our aging Honda Civic.

"What are you doing with that Mafia wagon, Herb?"

He looked shocked—he was never one to take a joke.

"That's a Mercedes, Alice."

"Beautiful," I said. For once, I hadn't meant for him to take offense. Reflected in the car's money-dipped flanks was a stocky woman in an out-of-style navy suit. I look a bit frayed around the edges, I thought and wished I'd gone ahead and driven the reliable truck instead of the temperamental Civic: Herb Rosen brings out the worst in me.

"The children will be taken care of," he said.

"Who's going to put them together again?" I asked. "How do you ask kids to get over something like this?"

Herb gave a little shrug. "I thought you'd want to know that I updated Max's will just months ago. Nothing was ever intended for Beverly. Most is for the children. A modest bequest to you as his literary executor—something else we'll have to discuss. Then there's some stock. I'd put it in government securities for the children's education. It's not enough to make a change in your life, but it will certainly appreciate enough to cover the state university. Perhaps something private if you have other resources. You'll need to move on it though. CATs maybe. We'll see. I can handle everything if you want."

I didn't say anything.

"You listening to me, Alice?"

"Yes, of course. But not today. I can't talk about anything today. I don't believe it, you know. I look around and I just don't believe it."

"Next week. Call and make an appointment any time. I'm in court Tuesday, that's all. For you, the week's free otherwise."

"You were his best friend," I said. "His lawyer, a professional adviser. Did you see this coming?"

"He was a bit nervous. But aren't we all? I don't know, Alice. I've asked myself that a hundred times since. I tell you, it's been a nightmare for me too."

"It doesn't make sense. None of this fits."

"It was Max, all right. Irrational, unexpected—it still happened. You've got to face that, Alice. The kids too, I know you want to protect them, but—"

"You believe this story?"

"I identified the bodies, Alice."

"That doesn't mean Max killed them. It just means they were killed."

"Who else? His gun, his cabin, no signs of struggle, close range—"

Doug and Julie and their grandfather were approaching, and I lifted my chin to warn Herb. "You've been a prince, Herb. I'll call you next week."

"Alice, take care." He kissed me again, inundating me with subtle, expensive scent: Max's best friend. Who believed everything. Which made me contrary and suspicious.

Chapter 2

M AX'S OFFICE WAS IN one of the older buildings on campus—a brick, cut-stone, and slate-roofed descendent of British collegiate architecture, complete with ivy on the walls and flowering trees in the courtyard. Inside, the Hughes Building was dreary and unimproved; the state had been miserly for years, and the history and political science building was far down on the glamour list that could expect renovation. Nonetheless, I had always liked Hughes, comparing it favorably with the sleazy fifties and sixties construction that disfigured the newer sections of the campus and the Branch. Max had had a fine square office on the second floor with a view over the lawns to the dairy barns of the agriculture division. His room was two doors down from the main department office, and I put my head in to thank his chairman and Stella, the department secretary, for coming to the funeral.

"I didn't get a chance to speak to everyone that day."

"Oh, Alice, how are you?" she asked, getting up and coming around her desk to kiss me. "I know what funerals are like." Stella was short and dark, with strong features and jet hair. "It's been such a shock."

"I should have come over sooner to clean out his desk, but I couldn't face it. His father asked me to sort the books, and I'm to handle any manuscripts. It seems that one of Max's last acts was to make me his literary executor.

She raised her thick eyebrows expressively. "No hurry. Though it's a nice office. There's a few who have their eyes on it already."

"I'll see everything gets tidied up today."

"You'll need the key," she said. "Of course, the police have been through it—twice."

I nodded. I didn't want to hear any more about the police, the details, the truth. I was beginning to be realistic, as Herb would put it, to be resigned. Doug was taking long walks with the dog. Julie shut herself up in the loft and played obscene lyrics by dubious bands. I was cleaning up, tidying away Max, trying to forget. On his door was a poster for a recent Scottish exhibition. Beside it was a card with Max's office hours and, taped to that, a handwritten notice that Professor Bertram's classes would be taken by Professors Giuliani and Carling until further notice.

Inside, the office was warm and dusty. The windows were closed, the blinds drawn, and Max or some careless investigator had left a plastic coffee cup on the desk. There were other posters along the walls from conferences and places we'd been, plus a reproduction Magritte showing a bland-faced man in a black topcoat who reminded me a little of Herb Rosen. I put the cartons I'd brought next to the bookcases and began going through the shelves. Stacks of undergraduate texts—largesse from the publishing hosts—could safely be left for the next occupant. The rest, the good history and political volumes, I packed before turning to the desk. It was littered with folders containing student papers marked in Max's tiny, neat writing: acerbic comments, exclamations, occasional bravos. I set these to one side for the department to manage, then picked up the leather picture frames with Doug's and Julie's pictures and stood remembering when and where they'd been taken: Julie on the horse, post-divorce, smiling at her father, a man she adored, who no doubt had been yelling, "Sit up straight! Look gorgeous!" until she started to laugh, her head back, hair flying. She

might one day be gorgeous; she had Max's looks. Doug with
the dog on the porch of our former house. Pre-divorce, this
one. He was squinting against the sun—probably exasper-
ating Max, who always craved enthusiasm—and clutching
the retriever's furry neck. I tried to remember if they had
always been so attached to animals or if it was only since
our marriage came apart. But that was treacherous ground
which I didn't want to explore. Neutral territory was safer—
like the neatly stacked chapters of what proved to be a history
of the Salisburys, the premier political family of the state.
The manuscript stopped after the Great Depression, and
when I checked Max's card files and found nothing on the
later members of the family, I went out and asked Stella.

"Oh, the Salisbury family history. About two-thirds done,
I'd say. Did you know that was commissioned?"

"I think Herb Rosen said something about it, but I wasn't
feeling too bright at the time. I'll have to get in touch with
the Salisburys. Was it to go right up through the Florida
senator?"

"As far as I know."

"That's odd. Max never started a book before all his research was finished. I didn't see any notes."

"I can't help you there." Stella compressed her lips as if
considering what she should say next. "Max, you know—well,
I probably shouldn't say this, but he hadn't been himself. He
was always so full of his own projects and ideas, but lately—"

"Lately?"

"Well, he'd been secretive. If someone said, 'How's that
article going' or something, he'd just say 'fine,' as if he didn't
want to talk about it."

"But he'd been busy on the book?"

"Oh, you know Max. He was at that word processor con-
stantly."

"Max liked secrets," I said. "In his personal life he liked
a lot of secrets."

"He was nervous too. Kind of on edge—as if something
was worrying him. Most of us thought it was just aftereffects. The divorce and all."

"He was living with Beverly Landis. Trouble there?"

Stella's expression was eloquent. "Up to his old tricks, I'm afraid."

"Anyone I know? I suppose I shouldn't ask, but old habits die hard."

"With Max too. There was a grad student—more than one, I think. And someone else. Yes, that was odd, really. What I mean when I say Max was nervous. A girl named Doreen came in and asked for him one day. Doreen Hale I think her name was. Just was he in and so forth. When I told him later I could see that he was upset. He went quite white."

"Doesn't sound like the Max I knew. What did she look like?"

"Oh, like they all look. No, that's not right. Flannel shirt, work boots. Either a forestry student or very liberated."

"Or worker?"

"No, student, I'm sure. She was carrying a backpack, notebook, pens, you know."

"Not pregnant and reproachful?"

"I wouldn't think so. She seemed very cheerful, as if she'd had good news."

"But not for Max." I picked up a carton of books. "Thanks, Stella. I'll get in touch with Len. I just—I just need to find out what went wrong for Max."

"Maybe you should talk with some of his students. They see things that we in the department—"

"Yes, I might. But if you should come across any of his notes for that manuscript—"

"—I'll be in touch."

"I was going to say 'or any answers.' "

"I'm so sorry," she said. "I really am."

I took her hand for a moment. "I know, Stella. It's the children. I haven't figured out yet how to explain to the children."

I left the office feeling puzzled and a bit depressed. A forestry student, nerves, and upsets: that didn't sound like insouciant Max, always after a beauty to share his scholarly interest of the moment. Instead, disaster and uncompleted projects. And from Max who'd always been so conscientious. That's what I told Vivian Salisbury a few days later. Mrs. John III, wife of the commissioning Salisbury, the last of a distinguished, if somewhat attenuated, line, and now established in the Sunbelt as GOP senator from Florida. Mrs. Salisbury was up north to oversee the renovation of that Connecticut landmark, the old Salisbury family mansion, and staying, until the dust settled, at the very plushy home of a friend in Glastonbury.

"Of course, we were terribly sorry," she said. She was a tall, attractive woman with prematurely white hair, a well-tended face, and enough tasteful jewelry to prevent her from doing anything more strenuous than opening the mail. Since the house looked as though everything was either automated or laid on by a large and silent staff, it was a match. "A tragedy," she continued. "And we'd felt Professor Bertram would do such a splendid job."

"What little I've had time to read is very interesting. Particularly the earliest period with Amos and Sarah in the wilderness."

"Farming, childbirth, Indians, and slaves," she said with a little shiver. "Max—Professor Bertram sent us some of the earlier chapters as he finished them. All those dead children," she said. "Poor things."

"I didn't realize you'd seen the manuscript."

"Just into the Civil War. John's quite the Civil War buff, you know. I'm not sure that he was totally pleased with the Civil War chapters."

"With the chapters or with the ancestors?" I asked. I'd done enough apologizing for Max's conduct without having to excuse Civil War magnates who'd dealt in shoddy and shorted the troops.

"Professor Bertram had promised to have the manuscript completed three months ago," she said. "If he'd made his deadline—"

"Inconvenient," I agreed.

"We'd promised the historical society."

I shrugged. "I can see about having the book completed if

you'd like. That's provided I can find his research notes."

"I'll have to talk to the senator," she said. "His own life, of course, has been covered so exhaustively."

Knowing campaign biographies, I agreed privately that that was *le mot juste.* "Well, let me know. We'd have to make some sort of financial arrangement, of course."

"Professor Bertram had been given an advance," she said.

"Professor Bertram, yes. But not me—or whoever completes the book. I'm sure you understand, Mrs. Salisbury."

"If anyone can," she said, but I'd already picked up on her way of changing a subject. "It was terrible. Just the most terrible thing. And for you, of course, even though—"

"Yes," I said, "even though." We shook hands, and she promised to be in touch. "But don't worry about the notes and things," she concluded airily, making me think that the mention of money had put her off. "There's so much on the senator that I'm sure we can find someone to fill in what Professor Bertram left. Send me some copies of the manuscript as it stands, and we'll take care of it."

I agreed to have copies made and left the acre or so of expensive carpeting, designer furniture, and *Metropolitan Home* ambiance that was her friend's living room. Three months late! That wasn't like Max at all. However casual he'd been in his personal life, he'd been almost obsessive about deadlines, and I couldn't help wondering if something had been wrong, something the autopsy had missed, some moral or emotional crisis hidden from his colleagues. And though I tried to put this thought out of my mind, it surfaced again during my consultation later in the week with Herb Rosen.

"I hope you aren't letting this eat away at you," he said. We had finished our business: the assets were listed, the children's funds earmarked, a broker selected.

I shrugged. "I still can't believe it. I won't believe it without some reason, some explanation."

Herb got up from behind his big desk, came around, and sat down on the edge of it. I noticed he was wearing beautiful shoes. "Listen, Alice, I'm the bearer of bad news first to last

in this. Max wasn't himself. Hell, we know that. None of
this would have happened if Max had been himself, but he
wasn't right before. It was little things—too many drinks at
dinner, missing appointments. He even told me he was having trouble concentrating. That scared him because it meant
he couldn't write. And you know Max was a slave to the
books."

"The poli-sci department secretary told me he was writing
all the time."

Herb gave a tight little smile, as if a cross-examination
were going to turn nasty. "Sure, he tried. But was anything
finished? Any disks? He wrote, then he wiped. He told me
everything was just garbage. Look what he was doing. A
commissioned family history! Was that Max's normal cup
of tea?"

I had to admit it wasn't. And I had to admit that Mrs.
John Salisbury III was probably not enough of a charmer to
account for his accepting the project.

"And even that was unfinished, I'll bet."

"About two-thirds done. Through the Civil War. Of
course, the family goes way back."

"More than I'd thought," he said. "But still. You've got to
face facts, Alice. I know, I know—if it was my kids I'd want
to say it's not true, there's some mistake, just like you. But
in the long run, reality's what you want for them."

"But whose, Herb? There's the question."

"This one's agreed upon. The inquest left no doubt." He
slid off his desk and picked up a key with a cardboard tag.
"I almost forgot the key for the cottage. Police have had it
sealed, but I'll call and check about it for you. You'll maybe
want to sell it. Whatever. But I'd advise you to wait a bit."

I turned the key in my hand, about to ask if we could have
the cottage cleaned and fixed up quickly. Then I changed my
mind. I'd had another idea, which I dismissed as morbid and
unwise but which pursued me through the week until Friday
morning, when, with the kids safely in school, I got in the
car and drove west. The cottage was not terribly far from the
University—Max lived there for a time after we'd decided to

separate—but it was well beyond the ring of country towns that served as bedroom suburbs for the university staff and faculty. Courton had a general store on the corner of the state road, a Congregational church with burial ground opposite, a Grange Hall, and a doctor's office. The cottage was off a narrow tarred road that didn't so much end as peter out, first to a dirt road, then to a potholed track that bounced up a short hill. The house lay nearly out of sight on the south slope: a dark, shingled building with a small barn that was gradually sinking back into the soil. There was a sheet of plywood over one window and a towel hanging out on the line. Below the house, a half-wild meadow extended to a stream, and from the hedgerow at its edge came a song sparrow's sweet, melodic call.

Max had bought this for me the fourth year we were married: an impulsive, impractical gesture financed by a little money from his parents and the surprisingly good sales of the book that had come out of his doctoral thesis. We spent the next summers repairing and reshingling. The building had never been completely finished, though it had been electrified. Max had been enchanted with the glow of kerosene lamps; afraid for the children, I'd held out for ordinary lighting. That had been emblematic; I'm not one for the romantic gesture. In a quarrel once, I'd asked Max why he married me. He said it was because I was reliable. Later I amended that: reliable up to a point.

A cloud passed over, the darkened grass bent in the wind. Down in the sunlight, a redwing began to sing. Though I used to love it here, I had not been back since I left Max. And if he had done this terrible thing, this terrible thing I did not wish to believe, the cottage was among the minor losses, the cottage and love and romantic gestures.

The towel was flapping erratically on the line, and, out of habit, I crossed the grass to unfasten the pins. When I turned back toward the house, I saw the fire damage, just smoke really. If the roof had caught, if the rain hadn't come—who'd have known the real story? Would there have been a search for bullets, for wounds? And why fire? A funeral pyre? It's surprising what the mind will and will not entertain. A shooting? Unlikely and unbelievable but conceivable. Then fire—too much. With that in mind, I felt realistic enough to put the key in the lock. It stuck, then turned. I pushed the door open and stepped inside.

The smell lingered—perhaps only in my mind: death. I stood in the front of the living room, swallowing. The floor had been wiped clean, though a chalk outline was faintly visible, and I forced myself not to look down. In any case, the floor was set over a dark and disagreeable crawl space. Damp and inaccessible. The loft was a better prospect—a wasp- and spider-occupied cavity that smelt of old shingles and dry wood.

I walked into what had been Doug's room. Through the adjoining door, I caught a glimpse of the bed, carefully stripped, where Bev and her son had been found—though he was seven, the paper said, old enough to have been sleeping in his own room. Before I could think it might have been Doug, it might have been Julie, I pulled over the straight wooden chair that used to hold my son's discarded shirts and fishing gear and used it to reach the trapdoor to the loft. Overhead, a sparrow fluttered out the louvered window, startling me so that I had to struggle to control my breathing. The cottage was full of ghosts, and any rustle, any shadow, was enough to give them form.

After a minute, I hauled myself up onto the splintery attic floor. There were cartons tied up with string, an old college trunk, a few eclectic piles of books. But though I switched on my flashlight, neither the cardboard boxes nor the trunk held any secrets.

I dropped back onto the chair and pulled the trapdoor closed. News reports and private conversations with the trooper in charge of the investigation had made it clear that the house had been undisturbed except for the carnage and that there was no sign of a robbery. Sensible enough: there were a half dozen new, expensive homes in the area and certainly nothing about the cottage suggested portable wealth. I decided to spare myself the rest of the interior and adjourned to the shed. A half hour there produced nothing, and tired and a bit dirty, I sat down on the front stoop to think about Max.

It is not exactly true that he had been evasive, but he had loved secrets, as well as buried treasure, maps, codes, hidden compartments, even egg hunts. When the children were small, he was forever organizing searches for Indian arrowheads, fossils, old nineteenth-century dumps with colored bottles. Max loved disguises too: Santa Claus, of course, at Christmas and a fantastic variety of homemade costumes every Halloween—dragon, witch, postage stamp, fur-covered Snoopy, crocodile. He'd missed his calling, which was, perhaps, to have been a prankish spy or a scholarly costumer. Reality had never been quite interesting enough for Max, who wanted alternate lives, alternate selves, alternate careers. He settled, as so many do, for alternate romances, for intense, short-lived affairs and academic flirtations.

I had always thought that if disaster came for him, it would come from one of his erotic adventures, from a jealous rival or from someone who did not see that charming Max was a creature to be enjoyed but not relied on: one's sentimental education, not the love of one's life. And, until those terrible moments, he'd picked wisely. I was the only one resentful; I was the only one who could not endure the humiliation; I was the one who had left him in bitterness and rage and sorrow. And since I was the one who had loved him, logic suggests—but I did not follow that line of thought to its lamentable conclusion. I am, after all, reliable and ordinary, not cut out for a crime of passion. If that's what this was.

I stood up and walked past the abandoned garden plot into the trees. The grass was surely tick-infested, and I was uncomfortably aware that I ought really to have worn boots. I would have gone back and been resigned and realistic, if I had not noticed the broken grass and bracken. Likely a deer trail—though there was no sign of the neat pointed hooves—or from Bev's boy, playing forts or Indians in the woods, like Doug, like Julie. I followed, nonetheless. The trail of broken grass bent toward the old well, and I felt a little twinge of excitement, even fear: Max might have left something after all.

The well had belonged to an earlier building, to the farm-house whose tree-choked fieldstone foundation lay moulder-ing just beyond a thicket of lilacs. Originally, the shaft had had only a flimsy wooden cover, which, after the children were born, we replaced with a heavy concrete tile and cap. I tried to shift the lid, but succeeded only in scraping my knuckles until I found a stick strong enough to act as a lever. The lid scraped back, then stuck as if it were caught on something, which turned out, after a good deal of heaving and swearing, to be an ordinary plastic dishpan, bolted onto the bottom of the concrete: a hiding place, such as Max had favored for amorous souvenirs and compromising correspon-dence. I was sure this device was since my time, and I felt a certain sympathy for Bev, my rival and replacement. The screws were loose enough to remove by hand and I unfast-ened the pan, expecting a handful of letters, perhaps photos— Max was an inveterate photographer even of clandestine affairs—and was surprised to find it empty. Had Max made this hiding place and died before using it? Or had Bev shown a precocious talent for detection? I knew perfectly well the other side of her lover's appetite for mystery: the late phone calls and missed dinners, the unexpected meetings and weekend conferences, the awkward silences at parties, the lies, but it had taken me a while. Years. Perhaps she had caught on sooner. I was considering that when I glanced down into the murky water glimmering faintly below the collapsed slats of the old well cover and saw something square, dirty, waterstained, and caught my breath. This time Max had been hiding computer disks instead of love letters. I wasn't sure what that meant, but I was oddly sure that I wasn't going to like it.

Chapter 3

Detective Crombie, the investigating officer, was young, intelligent, and pleasant: a perfect model for a trooper recruitment poster with a knack for public relations. "Mrs. Bertram," he said, giving a big smile, as if my arrival signaled a genuine pleasure instead of a sticky and time-consuming interview. He led me into his office, settled himself in his swivel chair, leaned back until the springs creaked, and smiled again. I had to admire him.

I produced the disk wrapped up in a couple of tissues. "I went to see the cottage today. Max's lawyer has recommended selling—for the children's education, you understand, and I thought I'd better—"

"Wise not to put it off," he said. He'd probably had courses in counseling: Grieving Widows I, Officious Ex-wives II.

"Max liked to hide things—secret compartments, false-bottomed boxes, that sort of thing. He didn't really trust banks."

"You'd be surprised at how many people agree with your former husband."

"Anyway, I thought I'd have a look around." My words felt like foreign bodies in my mouth: why was all of this so difficult? "I found one of Max's hiding places. He'd screwed a plastic container onto the cover of an abandoned well on the property."

Crombie poked at the damp tissue with the end of his pencil. "A computer disk."

"Ruined, I'm afraid. But I thought maybe your lab could resurrect something?" That sounded lame even to me.

"I doubt it. And what would be on it? You said your husband often hid things away."

"Yes, but letters, photos, memoirs of his secret life. Not professional papers and computer disks."

"Professor Bertram's behavior was consistent with a personality under stress," he said with the patient smile that, because quite genuinely sympathetic, was more irritating than rudeness or frank disbelief.

"Anything I point out as unusual gets interpreted as a sign of mental disturbance. That's the advantage of the diagnosis. Everything fits."

Crombie raised his eyebrows. "You said it, Mrs. Bertram. There's no way around that."

"But if there's no way your analysis can be proved wrong, it is not scientific. You realize that? It is Freudian, it is religious, but it is not scientific."

"Mrs. Bertram—"

I held up my hand. "You're busy. I'm a crank."

"No," he said gently, "you've had something terrible happen."

I felt tears in my eyes and jumped up and looked out the window. "If you just want to eliminate someone, you kill him," I said, getting hold of my wavering voice. "But if you want to eliminate and discredit him—"

"Mrs. Bertram, there's no evidence to support your contention that Professor Bertram, Mrs. Landis, and her son were killed by persons unknown. Nothing—physical evidence, forensic evidence, nothing—supports that claim."

"The bodies were badly decomposed."

"This is true, but everything we know now is consistent with the notion that Max Bertram was the perpetrator. For your sake, I wish it were otherwise."

"But why were Bev and her son lying on the same bed? Timmy was a child of seven. He'd been using Doug's old room."

"Who knows? As I've explained to you, there was no sign of a struggle, no sign the place had been ransacked. There's simply no motive. Besides, your husband—I should say your ex-husband—was a teacher, a scholar. Not exactly apt to be involved in dangerous stuff or to attract homicidal enemies, Mrs. Bertram."

"Not apt to turn multiple killer, either. And that's another thing. I didn't see the .22. Max used to leave it in the hall for rats."

"I believe we collected that. I'll check. If we did, it will be returned with his personal possessions."

"The funny thing is that he was a terrible shot. I wound up shooting most of the vermin."

Crombie gave me a look.

"Believe me, he would have to have practiced to have hit the side of the house."

"Well, he had time. He bought the gun in November. The sixteenth of November. We checked with the gun dealer. The salesclerk remembered that he seemed to know very little about guns. He claimed he wanted to take his son deer hunting. Apparently made quite a point of it."

"You'd wait a long time for Doug to shoot anything with four legs."

"Like I said, Mrs. Bertram, your former husband wasn't himself. But you let me check out that disk, all right?" He got up smoothly and ushered me to the door. Lt. Crombie was a nice fellow, but visits with him always upset me. I sat in the parking lot for a few minutes, feeling lousy, then had the evil inspiration to visit Warren Landis, Bev's ex-husband and fellow sufferer, a long-distance trucker who lived, I remembered, no more than a couple of miles from the state police barracks. I'd written him a note right afterward and had sent flowers to Bev's and Timmy's funeral, but I hadn't seen him. In fact, I had never met the man.

I suppose my only excuse was that I'd had enough of

reason, common sense, and business as usual. Half an hour
after leaving Lt. Crombie, the embodiment of all these good
things, I found a hand-painted wooden sign reading 'W.
Landis' on a dirt track leading off one of the narrower secondary roads. A good quarter mile in, the woods opened
around a large cream and brown house trailer, the cab end of
a semi, three cars in varying states of repair, and a handsome
pair of redbone coonhounds that immediately began to howl.
I parked beyond the reach of their lines and went over to
knock on the screen door of the trailer. When there was no
response, I called, "Mr. Landis?" The interior was dark from
the shade of the surrounding trees, but I thought I heard a
sound and called again. "Mr. Landis? It's Alice Bertram."

He appeared so quickly and silently that I was startled.
One minute I was peering into the dim interior; the next, a
heavy, unshaven face hovered an inch away from the screen.
"Yeah?"

"I'm Alice Bertram, Mr. Landis. I wrote you. I really should
have come to the funeral, but I—"

"Goddamn good thing you didn't," he said. His voice was
hoarse, disagreeable, and alcohol-cured. "You wouldn't have
been welcome."

"I guess I can understand that, but I'm sorry nonetheless."

"You should have kept that fucking bastard at home."

"Max and I had been divorced for several years, Mr. Landis. I didn't have any control over him."

"He had a wife of his own, didn't he? The goddamned
murderous prick."

"Max—"

"—killed my son. He didn't kill his own kids, did he? He
could have killed his own boy and you too, and left mine."
Behind the screen, his eyes glittered. I realized that he was
drunk and that this visit was a bad idea.

"I came to see you because I'm not convinced Max killed
anyone."

The door banged open then, so suddenly it caught my
shin. Warren Landis was a foot taller and conservatively
eighty pounds heavier than me. When he caught hold of my

arm, I wound up squashed against the aluminum side of the trailer.

"He shot them both. In cold blood. First he took my wife, then he took my kid. And listen, bitch, he owes me for both." Warren's eyes were bloodshot, fixed, and dangerous, and there was a nasty twitch at the side of his thin mouth.

"Max couldn't have hit a bus with a bazooka," I said, although I felt like crying. I'd been irritated by Crombie's confidence and Mrs. Salisbury's grandeur. But this was grief, crazy grief, not just Max grief, but Doug grief, Julie grief. "Goddammit, let me go," I shouted and pulled recklessly out of his grasp. "I was at the cottage just today! I know it could have been my kids! And I'm sorry, I'm sorry it was Timmy!"

He didn't say anything, but he didn't grab me again, either. He looked stunned, whacked out on misery, rumpled, unshaven, dirty. And there was something else: though he wasn't as handsome as Max, he was the same type, dark, with large, even features, a tall, powerful body. Max had been going soft with the professorial life; Warren Landis's downfall would be a combination of beer and sixteen-hour drives in the big rigs.

"I'm sorry," I said again and touched his arm. "I don't believe it, you see. I don't believe it, and I don't know what to tell my children."

"Tell them they're lucky to be alive," Warren said. "Tell them it should have been them." Then abruptly, he sat down on the step. "Shut the fuck up," he screamed at the dogs. They subsided into indignant barks, circling with their long, stiff tails in the air, and Warren Landis put his head in his hands and began to talk about his wife, "the faithless bitch," whom he'd, perhaps, owned more than loved and about Timmy, whom he'd neglected and adored.

"I was out with the rig, you know. Ten, twelve, fourteen hours at a stretch. Did she care? Did she fucking care? Always an angle with Bev. She wanted the money, but she wanted me home. Did Haulwel or Coast to Coast or Tomco Trucking give a fuck about that? Naw. They wanted the goods on the road. The freight delivered. I said to her, I said

I gotta damn well be able to rely on you. You know what she said to me? You know? She said I gotta live a little, Warren. With Timmy and all, I gotta live. She was living all right. With that fucking husband of yours!" He pounded the step with one large hand.

"Did you—ah—keep in touch with Bev?"

"Sure I saw her. Picked up Timmy regular. I paid support. I got Timmy every week. Let her deny that."

"And how did she seem?"

"Same as always, the stupid cunt." He went on in this vein, and though I heard quite a bit about Max and more about Bev, I didn't learn much. Warren's conversation fluctuated between reminiscence and threat, sorrow and rage, and all I got was confirmation of my original impression that the late Bev Landis was a conniver and a sneak and that, living with Warren, she'd maybe had her reasons. He swore and blustered and complained for what seemed forever, then, as abruptly as he started, he stopped and burst into tears. I was appalled by his mixture of malice and pathos. I wanted to run for the car and not look back, but I sat and talked to him for a while, and sometime after five he agreed to consider some coffee and, round about five-thirty, got himself up and went into the trailer. It was near six by the time I got home, feeling both shaky and thankful.

Doug was in the kitchen, white-faced.

"Dear, what's the matter?"

"Where've you been? I started dinner."

"I'm sorry. I had errands and then I stopped to see Mr. Landis. God, was that a mistake!" But Doug wasn't listening to me. I saw the tension in his face slide into anger and cursed my thoughtlessness. They both worried if I was late, if there was any interruption in the routine. At the same time, when I was home they were restless and quarrelsome, ate erratically, and shut themselves up in their rooms for hours on end. I put my arm around him. "You know there's a lot of business stuff. With your dad's affairs—" I felt him stiffen and pull away and knew it would be foolish to mention the cottage. "Where's your sister?"

He shrugged so elaborately that I was sure he knew perfectly well. "Dunno. She went out around four. When we knew you weren't coming home."

"As if I stayed out all night," I said lightly. "And Moira'll be around."

"Moira's out with that stupid ass Todd. She's not our mother! I didn't know where you were!" he shouted. "You didn't leave us a note!" His anger was frightening, almost out of control, then he turned and raced down the hall. The outside door slammed, and when I went to the back and called, I got no answer. He'd be back at dusk, refuse dinner, and go up to his room in a temper. Julie would be back when it suited her, which probably meant midnight or later, and I would probably have to ground her for a few weeks. With these cheerful thoughts and the sour memory of Warren Landis, I went to the pantry and poured myself a couple fingers of gin.

As it turned out, Julie was home by ten-thirty, full of studied indifference. She immediately overloaded the washer with a bale of clothing essential for her next appearance at school and blew the fan belt. I spent the next morning tracking down the local plumber, then went out with Moira and nervously potted up several dozen young thyme plants for the nursery while he examined the patient. Around eleven-thirty he came out smiling. "All set."

"You're a miracle worker, Sam."

"It'll do you for a while if you don't overload it. Those bearings look a bit worn."

"My daughter's a somewhat impetuous washer."

"Kids keep me in business," he said tolerantly.

"You have time for coffee and a sandwich?" I brushed the earth off my hands. "I was just finishing up."

"I have lunch in my truck, but I wouldn't say no to coffee."

"Good. Come on in. You want something, Moira?"

She gave me a look from under her straw hat. "Later, maybe. Thanks, Sam."

She didn't come in until he left, coffee, potato chips, and

apple pie later. "So how're you coming?" she asked.

"With what?"

"Romancing the plumber."

"I am not romancing Sam. Though come to think of it, I could do an awful lot worse. He's soothing, don't you think? And I like his gap tooth."

"He's sweet, sure. But he's a plumber. What would you talk about?"

"Max was a professor. As I recall, our conversation didn't exactly scintillate."

"I mean, be serious."

"I am serious. With plumbing like ours, we'd always have a lot to talk about. On a cold winter evening, I could fancy a nice chat about drains and elbow bends and the proper pitch for the soil pipe. I really could."

"Bullshit," said Moira, but cheerfully now. Moira fancies herself an intellectual, but her real province is matchmaking and unmaking.

"If you don't approve, don't put ideas in my head."

"Better than—" she said and stopped, biting her lip.

"—Max, etcetera," I said, finishing off the thought. "Amen to that."

"He's been on your mind a lot. I can tell."

" 'The manner of his passing' as they used to say, has imprinted itself."

She looked uncomfortable and I said, "I want to sneak off to campus this afternoon for a couple hours. Are you going to be home?"

"Sure. Just don't be late. I'm going out and I've noticed that Doug and Julie—"

"Yes. Sorry about last night."

"They're going to be anxious for a while."

"Me too. Thanks, Moira." I hustled outside and sprinted through my share of the weeding. At two-thirty I was in the car. Fifteen minutes to campus. Ten minutes' detour to deliver honey to the Tollards. Ten minutes to listen to the progress of the nasty rash that had lately afflicted Nan Tollard. Twenty minutes to track down the ramshackle multifamily that housed Pat Ryan, one of my late husband's doctoral candidates. Ms. Ryan was out back on a towel, risking her flawless pelt with a bikini and an aluminum reflector. A thick stack of books balanced the suncatcher, and she was making rapid notes on a stack of three-by-five cards. When I said hello, she jumped.

"I didn't mean to startle you." How can a whole generation be deaf at age twenty? "I'm Alice Bertram. I believe my former husband was your thesis adviser."

"Oh, Mrs. Bertram," she said, scrambling to her feet. "I am sorry. I mean about—what happened. Perhaps I shouldn't have mentioned that. He was the most wonderful teacher. Really the best I've ever had."

"That's very kind of you." She had a fresh, open face—rather, now that I think about it, like Sam—and she was totally unembarrassed. Nearly fifteen years of Max's infidelities had given me a pretty good instinct, and I was sure her relationship with him had been strictly educational. Well, well! Perhaps he had begun to settle down after all. Or maybe his interest was the ringer in the bunch, the chemistry maven, Doreen Hale. "Can I talk to you for a minute?"

"Oh, sure. Want to go inside?"

"The sun's nice—unless you're due to burn."

"I'll just put on my shirt," she said.

"You would have been in Max's graduate seminar?"

"Uh-huh. We did 'Topics in American Politics' this year. And before that, I took his Intro course as an undergraduate."

"What was the focus of Topics?"

"Money. Which turned out to be very interesting. I thought I'd find it dull—all those campaign finance reports and stuff, but Max had a way of making it fascinating."

"I'm told he was a good lecturer."

"Oh, yes. And he knew everything—environmental issues, the transportation industry—stuff way outside his field. But mostly we stuck to finance. It was even useful in a way."

"Oh?"

"I mean we came up with such a range of contributors—everything from IBM and GM to companies you'd never have

thought of like United Biologicals—that was my favorite,
they do school lab supplies—to mainstream insurance and
Florida developers. I may eventually go into business, and I
can tell you it opened my eyes. Besides, with the financial
disclosure acts in the seventies, there was a lot of material.
It was sort of fun to compare those later campaigns where
we pretty much knew the financial arrangements with the
earlier ones where we had to rely on letters and memoirs."

"Yes, I see. And Max—it's him I really wanted to ask
about. Did he seem—well, all right? Like you remembered
from your earlier course?"

"Oh, yes. He was marvelous. And so friendly and helpful.
We'd never have guessed there was anything wrong. We're
all still in shock. And so very sorry, Mrs. Bertram."

I thanked her and shook her hand. A pleasant young
woman and probably truthful. I doubted that I'd get anything more perceptive from Max's other students. Oh, yes,
the academic community who'd known Max would be helpful and considerate. What was depressing was the conde-
scension underneath, the 'poor Mrs. Bertram, he was
notorious, you know, obviously a symptom, and then—' To
tell you the truth, that's why I divorced Max. Whom I'd
loved. I could stand him; I just couldn't stand the pity which
is the lot of a plain woman married to a handsome philanderer. I couldn't stand the smug, glossy students, the sophis-
ticated professors, the bored faculty wives. One day I'd had
enough. I didn't give ultimatums, I didn't make a scene—
though to be perfectly honest, I'd made one earlier, a very
bad one. I don't like to think about that, about picking up
the old .22, about sliding in the clip, about Max's noncha-
lance turning to fear. How did I know he didn't kill Bev and
Timmy and himself? That look of fear, the fear of a dozen
civilized generations for uncivilized, murderous rage. Max
had been nervous about guns before; he was afraid of them
after. He certainly didn't buy a weapon to go deer hunting,
though maybe he had bought it for something else. And who
would know? Maybe Doreen Hale. I started the motor and
put the car in gear.

I nearly missed her dorm turnoff, slamming on the brakes halfway past the road and alarming an asphalt truck that had been tailing me. Ms. Hale was acting as resident adviser for a group of summer students, a wholesome activity that did not raise my hopes. But however awkward the situation, I needed to find Max's confidante, into whose shell-like ear my talkative adulterer would have poured his hopes, plans, and dreams of the moment.

"Can you tell me where I can find Doreen Hale?" I asked a tall, thin boy with a Carl Lewis haircut, a lime green singlet, pedalpushers, and sneakers so elaborate they looked like fungal growths. He was sitting on the stairs, all knees and elbows, with *Short Story Masterpieces* balanced on top of a basketball.

"Second floor, first door."

"Thanks."

I went up the concrete steps. Doreen's door was covered with cartoons and inspirational slogans: this crop of summer students were all foreign-born and inner-city, trying to get a leg up on the fall semester's work. I knocked.

"Just a minute. Oh, shit!" The door banged open. "Damn curling iron! I can't get—Oh, sorry." She waved the offending curler in one hand. "Expected one of my kids," she said. "Listen, I'm just on my way out."

Stella had not given me a particularly accurate report. Doreen was tall and shabbily dressed in a pair of cutoffs and a t-shirt. Her feet were bare and quite dirty. But the hair being curled was like a lion's mane, and she had fine, regular features and a quite spectacular shape.

"My name's Alice Bertram," I said. "I believe you used to sleep with my husband."

Chapter 4

"PERHAPS YOU'D BETTER come in," Doreen Hale said.

Her dorm room was walk-in closet size with the usual built-in cabinets and desk. The narrow bed was littered with clothes, shoes, books, and hair apparatus, but what caught my eye were a National Rifle Association decal on her bookbag and the large-scale topographical maps plastered on every wall. The title of the one nearest me was "Riparian Systems of Northeastern Connecticut."

"I thought you were a chemistry student."

"Environmental chemistry. I'm doing my thesis on heavy metals contamination."

"And Max? Forgive me, I'm not usually this heavy-handed, but where did Max fit in with heavy metal contamination?"

"Max fit in with the outdoors."

"With shooting?" I pointed to the decal. "You didn't by any chance teach him to shoot, did you?"

"No way. I'm on the U rifle team, but Max—wasn't interested." She looked disconcerted, then said, "Max was hiking, camping, and fishing."

"Out along the riparian systems of northeastern Connecticut?"

I recognized the Mashantucket forest. A trail had been outlined in red.

"Sure. The Quinnebaug river system, the upper Thames. Quite innocent."

"Nothing with Max was ever quite innocent," I said. But camping! Hiking! To the best of my knowledge, Max had never been fond of the outdoors. Even our summers at the cottage, which I think he secretly enjoyed, had been punctuated by complaints about the biting insects, noisy birds, and omnipresent mice. As for rural recreations, walking was pointless and tiring, shooting barbaric; fishing involved the disgusting job of gutting and cleaning, while birding was fit only for eccentrics, and botany, for old maids. Dogs were a nuisance, cats made him sneeze, horses were pretentious. The only good thing about the rural life was that it was conducive to reading. Otherwise, summers in the country were entirely for my benefit, a dispensation from his good will, a compensation for his infidelities—Max and I understood each other well in many ways.

"You're a bit late for a fight over Max," she said. Doreen had a strong jaw and a way of planting her feet that suggested she'd be tough to move.

"No quarrel over Max. He was very much my ex-husband. But he was my kids' father. I've been trying to figure out why things went wrong."

"I can't help," she said, but her eyes slid away from me in a way that made me sure she was lying.

"Max needed a confidante," I said. "Part of a long-term pattern."

"I wasn't the one," she said.

"And there's something else."

She had begun to fiddle with her hair.

"There's the fact that three people were murdered."

"Max killed them," she said quickly.

"But what if Max didn't? Then what?"

"That's nonsense."

"Is it? You knew him. Well enough, if I'm correct."

"All right. I slept with him. It was no big deal. Things were cool between Max and me but not serious. I just don't feel like talking about it."

"Weren't you surprised?" I asked. "When it happened, weren't you surprised?"

"Sure," she said. But she sounded uneasy rather than surprised.

"You must have formed an opinion. About Max."

"It wasn't that sort of relationship," she said.

"If you went hiking and camping with him, surely you knew whether or not he was a psychopath? Or was that part of the attraction?"

"Fuck off," she said. "I told you I don't want to talk about it."

I seemed to be losing my touch with the younger generation. "Don't talk about it then," I said, heading for the door. "But if I were you, I'd give it some thought."

As for me, I got in the car and was home like a proper mom with a pie in the oven before the kids returned. I spent the next few days in the garden, keeping ahead of the spring weeds and potting up plants for sale. Then, on Thursday, I was having a cup of coffee after several hours' work digging a new bed for herbs, when a short news story in the local paper caught my eye: "Hiker's Body Found." The deceased had been missing for over a month, and though friends assumed he'd gone on vacation, he had, in fact, been lying with his head bashed in some sixty yards off the popular Blue trail in the Mashantucket state forest. Although nothing definite would be known until the autopsy, the hiker appeared to have fallen from a basalt outcropping that was a well-known landmark and hiking destination.

The paper termed it a "tragic accident." For me it was an odd coincidence, odd enough so that the next time I was in town, I stopped at the sports shop to look at hiking maps and bought the one that I'd seen hanging on Doreen's wall. As soon as I got it home, I studied the trails and penciled in as accurately as I could the section that she had highlighted. When I was satisfied that I had reproduced the shape accurately, I checked the legend. Doreen and Max—if indeed Max had been keeping her company—had been roaming the area where the hiker had been found. Probably that meant nothing at all, but when a follow-up story raised questions about the hiker's death and his occupation, I began to feel both uneasy and curious.

On Saturday, I asked the kids if they felt like taking a walk. Julie had plans to spend the afternoon at a girlfriend's house, but Doug said he'd go if we could take Skipper. We loaded the retriever into the back of the truck and drove out along the state road to the Mashantucket. As we crossed several of Doreen's rivers running black and swift after the recent rains, I thought about her dissertation and about the popularity of bottled water and modern paranoia. Was some subtle contaminant the ultimate source of our fears and disillusionments, of violent angers and mass deaths—of whatever had happened at the cottage, of whatever had happened to Max?

The truck wallowed over the ruts in the parking lot, and in the back, we could hear the ecstatic retriever's nails rattling on the truck bed. I rolled up the windows, then watched as Doug put Skipper on the leash.

"Can we let him off farther up?"

"I think so. He's too old to wander off."

"Good old Skipper," he said. His eyes were like Doreen's, forever sliding away, but in his case, it was not deceit but the shock of existence. Doug seemed to want to catch life from the side, obliquely: he'd had enough surprises.

"I though we'd take the main trail," I said, unfolding the map. The track started from the back of the parking lot, rose several hundred feet, if I was reading the map correctly, then began a long descent toward the river.

"How come you've got a map?"

"I thought it would be nice to know where we were."

His look was sceptical, but he didn't say anything until he knelt down to unfasten Skipper's leash. "Dad had a set of maps."

"He traveled a lot."

"Maps like that."

"This one? Can you remember?" I could not conceal my interest.

"Yeah. So what?"

"I don't know yet."

"Is that why we're here?" He stopped on the path, troubled and wary.

"Yes and no. We like walking after all."

He didn't say anything more, but reluctantly followed Skipper, who, ever sensitive to tone of voice, had begun prancing nervously in front of us.

"I don't believe Max killed anyone," I said. "I've never believed that."

"No one agrees with you," he said. It was just a statement of fact.

"And you, what do you think?"

"I don't know what to think. Not since—"

"Since?" But I should have known what was coming.

"Since you guys split up," he said, his eyes fixed far down the path.

"We were both sorry about that," I said. "You know I loved your father, but I got so I just couldn't live with him. Maybe it was the same for him."

"There was Beverly," he said.

"Yes, there was Beverly and there had been others before Beverly. But that just makes him a poor husband. In other ways, Max was a fine person. Who wanted to do good things. Ambitious things."

"You really don't believe he shot them, do you?"

"No."

"So what are you going to do?"

"I think we're going to follow this trail all the way around the loop. Then I think we may go camping. That's what I think we may do."

"Are we looking for something? I could look too."

"Sweetheart, I haven't a clue. We just have to look, that's all."

The trail cut diagonally through the forest, past a public campsite, then across a swampy stretch so alive with mosquitoes that I guessed few pursued the path much farther. Once out of the marsh, it wound uphill quite steeply. At the last ridge, we stopped to catch our breath. Through the thin canopy of young leaves, I saw a bend of the river and the thin, dark line of the state road. I looked at Doug and he shrugged.

We had just started down the stony, circuitous track when Doug said, "Look, someone's had a campfire. That's not allowed."

"Good thing it's been wet. There's a lot of brush around."

Doug went over to poke about the ashes. "He had sardines. And candy bars."

The paper wrappers were faded, but still legible. I thought about the dead hiker. Tumbled from the rocks or, just possibly, struck on the head for reasons unknown. Was this his campsite? It was off the beaten track but very pleasant and possibly more easily reached from the river side. Which would account for the fact that no one had spotted him earlier, that no one had seen him entering the parking lot. Had he come by car? And if so, where would he have left it?

"You can see a cliff from here," Doug said.

I followed his finger. Through the trees was a pale gray spit of rock, crowned with saplings and bushes. Location of corpse.

I felt acutely uncomfortable. "Let's go back," I said. "We can't manage the whole thing today."

"Skipper needs a drink."

"Tell you what. Let's take the truck to the river. I'm sure there'll be a track in."

It took us nearly an hour to reach the parking lot, and the old retriever was panting heavily by the time I turned the truck off the state road onto a track near the water. Skipper bounded ahead to the river, splashed in, and began drinking noisily. Doug picked up a few pebbles to skim across the swift-running stream. I was enjoying this scene of bucolic tranquility—and looking about for trails leading up toward the rocks—when I heard a shout from our left. A man was emerging from the trees, shouting and gesturing, and accustomed to the friendliness of country people, I waved, then returned my attention to the water and to what now looked like a path leading away from the narrow county road bridge.

"Mom," Doug said, and I became aware that the man was

yelling angrily. Over the sound of the water and the dog's barking, I heard, "Clear off! This is all private property. I can have you arrested. That damn dog too!" He was carrying a short, thick rifle and didn't look to be kidding.

"Get hold of Skipper," I told Doug, for the old retriever was protective.

The man was tall and muscular with a dark mustache and a mop of dirty, streaked blond hair. His eyes were concealed behind mirrored sunglasses, and a Budweiser cap shaded his forehead. What little there was to see wasn't friendly, and I decided on complete innocence. "We thought this was all part of the state forest," I said. "We were looking to pick up one of the trails."

"No trails around here," he said, gesturing with the rifle. I noticed a red and black eagle tattoo across one wrist. "This is all private. So get off the goddamn property." As he spoke, Skipper began growling low in his throat. "Let that dog go and I'll shoot him."

Doug went pale, and I felt myself trembling with rage. "You point that weapon anywhere near my kid, and I'll be back here with the troopers and a charge of reckless endangerment and threatening."

"Lady, you're not supposed to be here," he said, but I could see that he hadn't liked the mention of the troopers.

"Our mistake. But if you don't want trespassers, post your land. Now put that stupid gun down so we can leave. Keep ahold of Skipper, Doug. I don't know whether this fellow wants trouble or not."

Our landowner had a pretty good line of invective, but the gun came down a few inches, and I nodded to Doug. Skipper barked and showed his teeth, but we hauled him safely past, and I took the leash out of my pocket and snapped it on the dog's collar.

A few dozen yards down the trail, I asked, "Is he still watching us?"

"Yes."

We passed through a screen of trees, and Skipper, feeling honor had been satisfied, shut up. I glanced back, but the man wasn't following and there was no sound of footsteps behind us.

"Mom."

I looked at Doug.

"He was lying."

"About?"

"This being private. I saw the state forest medallion on one of the trees."

"Unless it's a little bit that was surrounded by the park. There are probably some plots that were grandfathered."

"No," he said, pointing to a metal disk right at the side of the path. "And there's one on the other side too."

"That bastard!" I said, but the adrenaline was dropping. What I felt now was fear and relief and then fear again, magnified by Max and Beverly and her boy and the cottage and all the tensions of the last month.

"Are you all right, Mom?" Doug asked anxiously.

"As long's you're okay. You and Skipper." But my legs were shaking so much that I couldn't make myself climb into the truck. "I'm just being stupid."

"You were frightened," he said. An accusation.

"Of course. Did I fool you?"

He nodded.

"Him too, I think. A poacher, I suppose." I definitely wasn't going into anything more with Doug.

"But his eyes were troubled. "He wasn't a poacher."

"How do you know?"

"That was an M-1A."

"Maybe he's not a sporting poacher."

Doug shook his head. I sometimes underestimate my son. "No scope," he said. "Nobody'd use that without a scope for hunting."

$\triangledown$

Chapter 5

O N MONDAY, I HAD A fight with Moira. It had been coming for some time and was, in retrospect, a predictable result of a too casual division of labor, complicated by her romance with Todd Amiston, a shoreline restauranteur, and by the troubles that had followed Max's violent death. It started, as so many serious quarrels do, with a trifle: a printing snafu about labels for our honey jars. There was going to be a delay over some color work and the question was whether to stick with the plain labels we'd previously used or to wait until we could obtain the more elaborate and much more handsome ones that Moira had designed. The argument ended with mutual recriminations about skipped chores, poor delivery service, and work delays: all the griefs of a partnership going sour. Moira, who admittedly had gotten more than her share of the fallout of Max's gruesome departure, packed a case and announced that she was moving in with Todd. I was nasty enough to suggest that she'd be wise to check with him first and wound up with two weeks' worth of honey and three dozen flats of early lettuce to deliver.

I left the kids a note and loaded the truck in a foul mood. It was Max's fault from first to last. Without his chronic bad behavior, I'd still be an eccentric faculty wife with an unfortunate facility for candor. The kids would still be part of the suburban nuclear family that apparently comprised their idea of the good life, and I would never have watched a truck rumble down a county road with a group of laughing women in the back and thought there were other living arrangements, better lives, sounder designs.

But Max had hung around just long enough to screw up in such a spectacular manner that the rest of us would be dealing with the fallout for the rest of our lives. I was chewing this bitter cud and feeling put-upon and sorry for myself, when I pulled in for the last delivery at a little garden center near the campus. Though I should have returned home, I decided to see if I could raise any more of Max's graduate students, and I was in the department office, conferring with Stella, when Bob Giuliani breezed in.

"How good to see you, Alice."

"Hello, Bob. I'm afraid you've been landed with a lot of work since—" I was becoming squeamish, but there's really no delicate way to say "since my husband became a multiple murderer."

"Least of my worries! They were all well prepared. Max was always a stickler for detail, for preparation, documents, and citations. The Topics people have been a pleasure." He patted the ample cardigan that stretched over his portly frame and nodded his head. Although younger than me, Bob was already cultivating an old-codger air, suitable for the University professorship to which he aspired. "Yes, some very interesting papers, good, solid quantifiable material, though I don't know if you're concerned with that sort of thing." He started down the hall toward his office, still talking. "I must say I've learned something from picking up the course. Always imaginative, Max. Even with the undergrads who really are the dog work, don't you think?"

"I wouldn't know." Adjuncts never teach anything but freshmen or, in a pinch, sophs, giving me no basis for comparison.

Bob looked surprised, and he said something, though what it was I never discovered, because suddenly all my interest was focused on the bulletin board in the hall. There,

amid the layers of fellowship announcements, historical
journal prospectuses, grant deadlines, and conferences, was
a tattered brown on cream announcement: last November's
social history conference at the St. Louis Marriott, November 15, 16, 17. The day Max was supposedly engaging in
small talk with a local gun dealer and signing permit forms,
he was possibly safe in St. Louis!

"Were you at the last social history conference, Bob?"

"What? Oh, yes. Be a bit dry this year, though the sessions
on demographic data promise to be quite good. I'm presenting a short paper myself on—"

"No, no, last November's. The one in St. Louis?"

"—on population growth in eastern Connecticut counties
in the late Colonial period."

"Please think about Max for a moment, Bob! The one in
November. Did he attend?"

For all his dithering, Bob has an excellent memory. "He
took Wendy Sullivan's place. That's right. She'd gotten funding, then something came up that she couldn't go. Max
offered to read her paper."

"Max read a paper? What day? Though we can find that
out."

"Sure." He looked vaguely into his office. "I might still
have the program. They're handy for planning our state association meetings."

"Could you find it now? It's really important."

He shrugged, looking dubious, but decided to humor me.
"Let me see." He began to paw through the piles in a cardboard box labeled 'Conferences' in big red letters. He seemed
to have attended a lot, planned almost as many, and I got a
running commentary on both before he held up a thick program. "Here we are. 'Women Factory Workers under the Family System in Nineteenth-Century Connecticut and Rhode
Island.' Wendy Sullivan."

"Wonderful. And do you know where he stayed, Bob?
Would he have been at the Marriott?"

"Yes, he was. Because we shared a cab in from the airport.
Though he was on a different floor. I'd taken a suite because

I had students lined up to interview. It's so hard to get any who really understand the quantitative approach to historical data."

"There'll be records," I said. "Even if he paid in cash, there should be records."

"There are always records," he said. "It's a matter of knowing what constitutes a record and how a record ought to be interpreted. That's been my strength—interpretation. One needs—"

"I'll need to copy this," I said, taking the booklet out of his hand. "You've been terrific, Bob. Max would have appreciated it."

"I'll need that back," he said, but I was already at the office door, waving to Stella and heading for the stairs. Outside on the pink-and-white-blooming quad, I caught my breath and looked again at the conference program with its boldface type. No one had thought to double-check! They'd been so sure that the question had never even come up.

I'd caught Detective Crombie at lunch: ham and cheese on rye, side order of fries, two pickles, and a danish for dessert. With coffee. Not the best for his heart and lacking in fiber. Insufficiently herbal and natural—he was clearly not one of our customers. Once I'd have apologized for disturbing him. Now, I was secretly glad. No one had been very helpful when Doug and I reported the "poacher." Thirteen-year-olds aren't supposed to know gun calibers, and when nothing much can be done, members of the public are to be soothed and subtly discouraged. I laid the conference notice on his desk. "Max was in attendance last November. You'll notice the dates?"

"He was there for the whole time?"

"Came in on the Thursday night, the fifteenth, with a long-time colleague. Left on Saturday." I added two more pieces of paper. "The hotel faxed a duplicate of his bill. And I checked the airline schedules. There just isn't any way he could have gone to St. Louis on Thursday, returned to Connecticut on the sixteenth to buy the gun, and still have been back in St. Louis to read Wendy Sullivan's paper on the afternoon of the seventeenth. That's why he went, when he wasn't scheduled to go. I checked with her. She said she'd gotten a lot of requests for offprints from people who'd heard the paper."

"So," Crombie said.

"So, someone went to an awful lot of effort to buy a gun in Max's name. Leading me to believe—"

"Perhaps the dealer made an error. Got behind on his paperwork, fudged a bit, got the date wrong. Isn't that a simpler explanation?"

"Simpler, but not necessarily correct. Simpler if you believe Max killed Bev and her boy and himself. Not simpler if you believe someone else killed all three."

He gave a tired smile. That heavy protein, fat, and sugar diet wears you out after noon. But he could discover that for himself.

"Will you check with the dealer?" I asked. "To see if there was some error, some omission?"

"We'll take care of it."

"Because otherwise I'll go myself. You can keep those—I've got copies."

"Mrs. Bertram, as I've tried to explain, the case is officially closed."

"And that other matter? My son and I were threatened the other day. In the Mashantucket, where just incidentally, Max and his latest girlfriend used to go hiking. Max, who never liked the outdoors."

"The park rangers have been warned to patrol the area more regularly. Almost certainly the man who accosted you was a poacher who panicked. You cannot keep seeing everything as connected to what happened to your ex-husband, Mrs. Bertram."

"Only a very stupid poacher would come out of the woods, walk several hundred yards carrying a high-powered weapon, and alert people to his whereabouts."

"You'd be surprised, Mrs. Bertram. You'd be surprised at what we have to deal with." He stood up.

"What about the hiker? Has that case been officially closed as well? The hiker who was found—oh, I'd guess a mile, two miles from the river where we met the poacher?"

"That is still under investigation. You should know I cannot comment."

"And by the way, did you find his car? If I were you, I'd look in the area south of the rock, along one of the tracks beside the river. Those provide easier access to that part of the forest than the trails from the parking lot. Convenient but maybe not smart."

"Why do you say that, Mrs. Bertram?" I should have paid attention to the question, because the detective rarely asked for amplification.

"Because camping there was perhaps what got him killed," I said. "He didn't come with a kid and a dog. Or maybe he was the belligerent type. Like Max."

"And like you, Mrs. Bertram?"

"Only when I lose my temper, Detective Crombie."

On my way out, the wind caught the door and gave it a satisfying bang that made the other officers and the desk staff look up. To hell with them. But I had something concrete. A date, a time. Let them prove there'd been a mistake. And I had a place. Tonight was Doug's night for swimming. I decided to pay Julie for some potting up and to visit the forest after dropping Doug at the pool.

"Will Moira be back?" Julie asked when I broached the subject. Though they wouldn't admit it, the kids were nervous. Doug had called me into his room one night about a car parked along the road, and Julie jumped every time the phone rang.

"Moira's staying with Todd. I think she was beginning to find communal life taxing."

"Me and Doug, you mean."

"No. If anything, me and everything that's happened."

"She doesn't like my working."

"This will be between you and me. I'll pay you directly. Off the budget. All right?"

"Yeah, sure. But I've a chem test tomorrow."

"Study for that first, then pot instead of getting on the phone and running up the bill. It's important"—I caught myself—"that you do well on your exam. Next year you'll be looking at colleges."

"If I decide to go."

"And if you don't go, you'll be working as low-paid farm labor," I said as cheerfully as I could, "so you'll need to be good at potting up."

"You wish."

"No, I don't wish."

She began pushing a line of dirt along the potting shed bench with a bundle of plastic labels.

"You'll get those dirty."

She kept steering the earth into a triangular pile. "Where are you going?"

"Just out birding."

"You're going back to the state forest," she said.

"One of the best places for warblers."

"Doug says you saw someone there with a high-powered rifle."

"That was odd, wasn't it?"

She nodded, and her face was so serious that I felt she was entitled to a little more.

"Also, your dad used to walk there."

She looked up quickly, half-sullen, half-hopeful. She had idolized her father and could neither accept what had happened nor the worth of her memories. "So what?"

"I don't know. I don't know why he got interested in hiking all of a sudden."

"Interested in some woman," she said.

"Hmmm," I said and hoped to leave it at that.

"They say he went crazy."

"You'd just seen him. Did he seem crazy?"

She lifted her shoulders. "No," she said after a long silence. "No, he seemed the same as usual. Maybe a little nervous."

"Maybe he had a reason to be nervous. I don't know, but I don't believe what everyone says. So I thought I'd have a look around. I think we owe it to your dad to keep an open mind."

She didn't say anything, but her expression told me she'd taken the idea under advisement.

"If you have time, pot up some of that young lavender and the parsley," I said and went out to the car.

Skipper was barking and jumping at the end of his rope, but he was too old and basically too friendly. For the first time, I wished we had something more formidable, a rottweiler, a dobie, or a mean-tempered shepherd. Even Max's old .22. But that was melodramatic, and Detective Crombie had assured me that such wishes were a product of grief and paranoia. Well, we'd see. I planned to abandon the kids for the evening and put his theory to the test.

It was a soft, still evening with one of those high, clear skies that are becoming all too uncommon. I left the car near the bridge on a dirty turnoff much used by fishermen, took my binoculars and walked along the verge of the state road until I reached a track leading into the forest. After a few minutes, the traffic was muffled. Chickadees whistled and called overhead, higher still, and in the branches, came the thin, soft twittering of the spring warblers. Though the migratory flight had been on for a couple of weeks, I'd not yet gotten out with the glasses, and forgetting that I was on serious business, I raised the binoculars to a patch of lemon sky and tiny, opening leaves. A small bird was fluttering along one of the branches, a little brown, white, and yellow creature half hidden by the tender chartreuse of the young oaks. The low evening light caught a flash of cinnamon: the chestnut-sided warbler. Yes, and there was his call, the heavily accented *How, How, How are you?* Good question.

The answer was, better now. Another source of contention between Max and me had been our social temperaments. Max had been sociable to a fault. I need to be alone on a fairly regular basis, in places like this where trees tremble with small jeweled birds. Overhead were myrtle warblers with their yellow rumps and a few elegantly striped black and whites. I stopped moving the glass and fiddled with the adjustment, trying to bring one darker bird into focus. There was a flash of orange-gold and a greenish back. I was thinking, a wood warbler, when I stepped sideways in hope of a better view and felt my ankle go over. I dropped the glass, put my hand down to break my fall, and wound up on the leaf-strewn track that any fool not occupied with the treetops would have seen was cut by a pair of deep tracks. Someone had brought a truck through this part of the wood over the old logging road that crossed the path. The nearby ruts were new—another run and this trail would be impassable—but the rest of the intersecting road was old blacktop, leaf strewn and stained from treads of other vehicles that had wallowed off into the soft forest floor, mistaking the way.

Reluctantly abandoning the birds, I followed the road, which shortly turned straight toward the water. Trucks had come down here to the river. Across the way was the hiker's rock and, if I was right, his campsite, accessible by crossing the bridge. Our poacher had emerged from the trees at the edge of the meadow opposite. I walked to the edge of the river, which was flowing clear and swift, a dark sheet with a sheen of pink evening light across the ripples. It smelled like fish, like weeds, like ordinary water. I dipped my hand in, but there was no oil sheen. Behind me an ovenbird gave a nervous, rising interrogation. What had this to do with Max?

The forest was dark across the river, and the pink sunset was dulling as I started back, intending to pick up the trail to the highway. The light failed so rapidly, however, that I didn't notice the intersection, and by eight-twenty, I knew I'd missed the shortcut. I was going to be late to pick up Doug, and I was fussing about that, reproaching myself for not having brought a flashlight, when I heard the broken hum and whoosh of cars on the county road. I'll be on time after all, I thought, and started to jog. I was puffing along, hoping to avoid too many questions about my evening drive, when a wall of light struck the trees to my left. A roar exploded from the softer sounds of the highway, and the whole road was filled with a triple tier of lights moving at frightening speed. I jumped off the crumbling blacktop, bounced into a cluster of bushes and brambles, and stumbled behind the trunk of a tree as a spray of dirt and gravel rattled through the leaves. The truck went by, big as a house, then I heard the whine of hydraulic brakes, a shout. The vehicle came to a halt in a swirl of lights and dust, but before I could make out any name or plate, I heard footsteps pounding on the road, and without stopping to think why, I scrambled into a tangle of sumac and young saplings. Beyond was the soft darkness of a grove of hemlocks. I dove under a low-hanging branch and slid behind a tree. So long as I was quiet I was safe, for the truck's powerful lights, silhouetting the brush and trees near the road, would blind anyone looking toward the darkness. Then a flashlight beam swept over the foliage, and I dropped flat on the ground. Almost instantly, I felt ridiculous: a melodramatic paranoid. They had stopped to see if I was hurt; they had been surprised to see a hiker so late. Possibly they were people I knew, gone fishing after hours in the company truck or the hay wagon. A voice would say, "For Christ's sake, Alice!" And what the hell would I say to that? Before it was too late, I should stand up, shout. Ask what they were doing here so late. So quiet.

Then I realized that my instinct had been correct. If you're afraid you've hit someone, you call. These people were quiet. They weren't worried about my welfare at all, they were worried about my existence. My breath became a reverberant wheeze. The light played on the branches a few yards to my left. Would they venture in? If so, I'd better risk the noise. I couldn't stand the thought of lying, waiting, listening to footsteps, snapping twigs. But maybe they weren't coon hunters and country people. Maybe they were city folk, nervous about ticks and snakes and irritated by the clouds of mosquitoes that even now were at work on all the exposed portions of my anatomy. A minute more. I punched the button on my watch: 8:35. Doug would be out in front of the Y pool in twenty-five minutes. Ten minutes to the highway, a half hour to town—if I could risk walking back along the road.

Soft voices came from the road. A conference. Then footsteps. Two? Just two. Had there been more? I heard the truck
shifting gear, the rumble as it pulled away, and stood up
cautiously. It was dark in the hemlocks, but with the truck's
blinding lights gone, there was a faint pink-gray tinge beyond
the sumacs. I needed to go southeast to hit the road and the
distant sounds of the cars would guide me. Ten minutes of
daylight, no more. I started further into the trees, but even
with the sound of the cars, faint over the peepers and tree
frogs, I soon found myself uncertain of the way. The forest
floor was strewn with rocks and stumps, and the land beyond the trail pitched down into a steep gully. In a few moments it would be totally dark, and when I heard the truck
returning, I wasted no time turning back and beating my
way through the brush toward the blacktop. His lights
swung through the trees, giving me a clear idea of my location. Then I heard the engine slow for the highway, and I
stumbled through the brush to the paved road. It was already
eight-forty-five, but out of the woods I'd make better time,
and I started to run, binoculars in hand. The pool was not
in a good section of town; Doug would be waiting outside.
Around his image nameless, irrational fears rose like a flock
of starlings before I saw lights on the road and sprinted forward, panting. On the verge, I stopped, looked both ways,
but there was nothing, no flashlight, no parked truck, no
one loitering near my car. All was as safe and ordinary as
Detective Crombie had promised, and sides aching, I ran to
my car, threw the glass inside, extracted my wallet from the
glove compartment, and started the engine.

Five miles down the road, I pulled into a seedy little tavern
frequented by bikers and truckers, and parked the Honda
between a pair of hulking vehicles that seemed newly sinis-
ter. A man was just leaving the smoky phone booth in the
foyer, and I nipped inside, put a quarter in the slot, and
punched up the YMCA number. "The pool office, please."

"I'm sorry, the pool closes at nine."

"This is Alice Bertram. My son is in the evening swim
program . . ."

Sympathetic sounds. The invention of a failing battery. Would be delayed. The offer of a ride from Tim Hong's mother. Apologies, gratitude. I hung up the phone, and as my anxiety lifted, I glanced at the interior of the tavern. The pool table was in use, several tables were occupied, and there was a smattering of patrons at the bar, one of whom was Warren Landis. Though there shouldn't have been any surprise in that, the sight of him gave me an unpleasant feeling, and I was still standing at the door of the phone booth when a tall fellow with a trucker's hat and mirrored sunglasses stepped up impatiently.

"Sorry," I said and stepped aside. He grabbed the door handle, giving me a glimpse of his wrist, thick with blond hair and a red and black eagle tattoo.

Chapter 6

THE ONLY GOOD THING about Thursday was that the
kitchen sink stopped up: it was that kind of week. Doug and
I had a nasty argument after swim night—a product of
anxiety on both sides—and we returned home to find one of
Julie's boyfriends ensconced in front of the TV, beer in hand.
By the time the dust settled from the explosion that followed,
we were into the wee hours, and I got up Thursday morning
in an uncharitable mood. Moira arrived at 8:30 to find me
still at breakfast, though I am usually at work an hour and
a half earlier—as she well knows. The sense of her moral
superiority that hung over the morning did nothing to
improve my temper, and it was lunchtime before I could
bring myself to ask, "So how's life chez Todd?"

"Chez Todd is fine, thank you."

"That's good. He seems a nice fellow."

"Yeah. Listen, Alice, we've just got to talk."

"All right." When Moira's "just got" to talk about anything, it's usually bad.

"We're getting married."

"Moira, that's super! I hope that you'll be happy."

She put her arm around me. "It hasn't come at the best
time, I know."

"Don't worry about us—unless you want to dissolve the

farm. I don't have the capital to buy you out. As you've probably guessed."

"No. In fact, I think we'll acquire another customer. Todd's gotten interested in fresh veggies, herbs, goat cheese. He's very health conscious and wants to educate his clientele."

"I'm all for that."

"It's the house that's the problem. It ought to be in your name now, and we ought to incorporate the business properly. Especially if I'm married."

"God knows what the shack's worth the way property has gone up. I'll have to talk to Herb, Moira, and see if I can borrow against the kids' money or something."

"Todd said something about getting it appraised."

"Todd's the soul of business. Maybe you'd want to arrange that? And the land. Am I to own the land? If so, are we still fifty-fifty? We'll need to talk to a lawyer." God! Do I need this?

"I could do the deliveries today," Moria said, "and go on into town if you can do the milking."

"I may have an errand to run later, but it's no problem."

"You're still on mysterious errands?" She clearly didn't approve.

"Not mysterious really—I'm trying to bury Max. I thought I was all through with him. I thought that I was at the point where Max was nothing more in my life than someone who picked up the kids on alternate weekends."

"And now he's dead," said Moira. "You might be realistic and start to get on with your life."

I hate phrases like "get on with your life." As if one could take a break and say, Give me a little time, I'm not ready to get on with life just now. "Getting on means finding out what happened to him."

"Hmmm," said Moira. "But you'll contact your lawyer?"

"I'll give Herb Rosen a call. He's very big on being realistic."

"You don't have to be sarcastic," said Moira. "There just comes a time to be businesslike."

I told her I'd keep it in mind, and I was certainly business-

like about Doreen Hale. The first time I called, she hung up
on me. The second time, she said something creatively obscene. There was no third time. Instead, I phoned Ted Friedland, a water pollution specialist I knew at the University,
on the pretext of doing an article about the state's endangered waterways. He turned out to be one of Doreen's advis-
ers, and the next day I was turned over to her—or, more
accurately, she was turned over to me—as something of an
expert on eastern river systems.

"That was pretty dirty," she said, when Professor Friedland left the room. "I don't know why I should tell you a
goddamn thing."

"You should, because otherwise I'll raise hell with Friedland. Listen, I told you I had to see you. One reason's for me,
but one's for you."

"I doubt that," she said.

"I need to know where you were collecting samples—in
particular, if you were in the Mashantucket state forest."

"I took samples along the entire Thames river system and
its tributaries."

"And the results?"

Doreen gave a put-upon sigh, but once she got started,
her interest in the subject got the better of her. "Pretty predictable. There's a lot of heavy metal pollution once you get
into the industrial belt. Rather high readings for lead and
cadmium near the Sound and a considerable presence of
mercury too. Let's face it—the water quality sucks down
there. There's bacteriological contamination, phosphate
and pesticide residues, not to mention the various organics,
including—"

"But up north," I said, interrupting. "Around the forest?"

"Pretty clean overall. You do get traces, of course. For one
thing, from the combustion of leaded gasoline. That was
basically the point of the study—to develop a baseline, to
look at both relatively clean and quite heavily contaminated
waterways."

"I noticed the map. The map of the Mashantucket with
the trail highlighted."

"So?" I couldn't say how she did it, but Doreen conveyed a sullen indifference as well as anyone I've met.

"I went there the other day. Down along the river, a nasty fellow with a high-powered rifle informed me that I was on private property. Which was quite clearly a lie."

"You get all kinds of nuts," Doreen said.

"Amen to that. But it puzzled me. Enough so that I went back two nights ago. I was on the south side of the river, walking on the old blacktop road. Do you know the one I mean?"

"Yes." She seemed a shade more interested.

"Just at dusk, I was very nearly run over by a big truck that came barreling in off the main road and, get this, stopped to see where I was."

"What's so surprising about that?"

"They didn't make a sound. They didn't call, they just swept the woods with a flashlight—then went roaring off. So that's why I wondered what was going on there. Why I thought I ought to warn you, especially since the hiker was found dead."

"That was an accident," Doreen said too quickly. "He apparently fell climbing."

"Maybe," I said. "You'll notice that hasn't been definitely established. I'm going to ask you again if you found anything or if Max knew anything—and don't tell me how he loved the outdoors. That's a crock."

"I've told you everything," Doreen said. "Here's a copy of my data, if you don't believe me. Very low heavy metals. Toxic dumping they're not."

"I was wrong, then," I said getting up. "But I'd stay away from the river if I were you."

She gave a quick, cat's smile. "I'm not a crusader," she said.

"And Max?"

"Max lived a fantasy life."

I could agree with that, though she'd told me more than she knew: Max *had* been after something. But what? And why the truck? I put the pieces together in a half dozen different combinations on the way to Herb's office and didn't like any of the permutations. Unconvincing, somehow. Like Herb's concern for me.

"So, Alice! Good to see you." He kissed me on both cheeks. Perhaps Herb is a sublimated philanderer. "You're looking pretty well."

"Try harried."

"The curse of modern life."

There was a little more such persiflage before he smiled and sat down behind his immense desk. The wood was like the best moiré silk with a swirl of darker grain. Time for business. "You need money," he said.

"I need money. The farm is self-supporting and looks like a pretty good business. But, understandably, Moira wants her money out of the house. If she's not living there."

"House and land go together?"

"They did when we bought the place, yes."

"We'll want to get both appraised."

"Moira's seeing to that, and I have the original figures. The house and the main barn have had some work."

Herb nodded and began making notes on one of his yellow legal pads. We discussed types of partnership agreements and various percentages of ownership in house and land.

"There's your bequest. That is yours free and clear."

"It's not quite enough, though, is it?"

"Probably not. And even with borrowing against your equity in the house"—he shook his head—"it would still be tight."

"I was wondering if I could justify borrowing some of the children's capital. It is their home, and the business provides their maintenance."

"That's doubtful, Alice. As trustee, I'm obligated to do my best by their property. Note, I said 'their property.' Not even necessarily what would be best for them—which, in this case, would almost certainly be staying in the home they're now used to."

"But it's not completely out of the question?"

"No, not completely. I'd have to consider your other assets very carefully. You understand."

"Yes. I'm again in your debt, Herb."

"I told you—anything." He stood up, beaming. "And you, Alice," he said as we walked across the expanse of polished oak and Chinese rugs to the door, "really, how are you doing?"

"All right. Considering."

"Did you ever hear again from the Salisburys?"

"Mrs. Salisbury seemed put off by the idea that I'd want to be paid to finish the manuscript."

"That's Vivian, all right. Poor Max." He shook his head regretfully. "He left us just before John got really interesting."

"Don't let partisanship cloud your judgment, Herb. The day John Salisbury's interesting is far off."

"You think? I know different. John is going to be in the race next time. I know that for a fact."

"The race?"

"For the presidency, Alice."

"You've got to be kidding! He's handsome and pleasant but clever he's not."

"It doesn't always do for a candidate to be too intelligent, you know. He's got the common touch."

"With the Salisbury millions? Come off it, Herb. Pick another horse!"

"You liberals are all alike, Alice. People don't want someone in your image. You'll see."

"Well, good luck to him. I'll pray for the Republic."

"Good luck to you too, Alice. Maybe you'll surprise Vivian and find those notes."

"Well, I've been looking but all I've found so far is one soaked computer disk."

"A computer disk?"

"Max had a hiding place for it at the cottage."

Herb's face changed subtly. "A hiding place?"

"Unfortunately, it had been emptied out—except for the one disk. You know how secretive Max was."

"Yeah. Secretive as hell. I still miss him." Herb compressed his lips and shook his head. "Listen, Alice, I'll try to find you some money. And if you find those notes, let me know. I'll handle Vivian for you. I don't think literary deals are going to be your forte."

I thanked Herb, got home by five-thirty, had dinner ready for the kids at six-thirty, and was looking at a flooded sink by seven-fifteen.

"I'll get the plunger," Doug said, and dashed toward the back door. He's getting used to the tools and improvisations of rural life.

"Never mind," I said. "I'm going to call Sam. Even if we get it opened, there's something wrong. It's on the blink far too often."

"I'll just give it a try."

"You'll have water everywhere," I said, and went to the phone.

"Mom wants an excuse to call Sam," Julie said in a superior tone. My daughter can be uncomfortably acute at times.

"That back lawn needs mowing," I said. "You two could get on with it."

"I'm supposed to study chemistry."

"I've heard that one before. Lawn first. Doug can do the raking and run the weed eater. You handle the mower."

Their protests were immediate but halfhearted. Both of them like machinery and neither minds outdoor work so long as it involves something noisy. As the screen door banged shut, Sam came on the phone.

"Sam, it's Alice Bertram. I'm sorry to bother you, but the sink is clogged again. I'll plunge it, but could you stop by in the morning?"

"May need more than a plunge," Sam said.

"I'm afraid there's tree roots or something."

"Most likely. That damn willow. Why don't I stop by in a little while?"

"Well, if it's not too much bother—I'll see if I can get it cleared in the meantime."

I hung up, scraped the dirty dinner plates, washed them in the dishpan, and threw the soapy water outside. Then I put the plunger on the drain. It uttered a series of mournful belches and dislodged a cloud of brownish waste. The sink began to empty sluggishly. What would cleaning the line cost? Or replacing the piping? All this on top of buying Moira's share of the house! I couldn't manage it unless we had an awfully good summer season. The best ever. Anything less and I'd have to look for full-time work somewhere, and that meant a delay on the greenhouse we'd planned and another year before the business turned a decent profit. Which it had to pretty soon. Julie would be ready for college in two years, Doug in four. Very soon I'd have to decide whether I was sticking it out here or taking a full-time teaching job—assuming I could get one.

Only the sound of Sam's truck outside enabled me to put those disagreeable reflections to one side. I ducked into the hall, consulted the mirror, and ran a hand through my hair: no point in always looking disheveled.

"Come on in," I called. "Hi, Sam. I've got it open, but just barely."

"Better than nothing. Rest of the drains okay?"

"God, I hadn't even thought about that! I'll check."

"You'd probably have noticed something."

"Lately, I'm not too sure," I said. I went into the lavatory, then up to the bathroom and turned on the taps. "Seems all right," I said.

"I think it's just this line. We'll see. Third time lucky, maybe."

"One of those days?" I asked.

"I just got home. Sometimes I think I'd like to see what nice, new, modern plumbing looks like."

"And where would you be, if we all had nice smooth-running fixtures?"

"True enough." He emptied the trap, then inserted a long flexible metal strip into the lower part of the drain. "Ah. That seemed to help."

"Saved from a major job?"

"Looks like it."

I couldn't help a sigh of relief, and Sam turned from washing his hands at the sink and smiled. He is wiry and well knit, but not really large. A lot of his work is heavy, and he looked tired. I said. "Have you time for a piece of pie and coffee?"

"I'd love it, but I ought to go home and eat dinner."

"You can have that too, if you don't mind cold chicken and potato salad. I'd just put them away before I called you."

"I don't want to trouble you—"

"It's no trouble," I said, setting a place for him. "I should have waited till morning. You want coffee or iced tea?"

"Coffee's fine."

"The kids are big on iced tea. Sometimes I just feel like sane adult company." That was a non sequitur, but Sam seemed to understand. Despite his open, unmarked face and cheerful disposition, he'd had his share of bad times. As I had the story, his marriage had broken up while he owned a fair-sized plumbing and heating business. He'd sold it in an attempt to spend more time at home, but things still hadn't worked out. The wife was remarried somewhere, their daughter came for weekends, and Sam was rebuilding his business here in the low-rent district. His sweetness and calm were either hard won or a bit deceptive.

"You're a good cook, Alice," he said when he was finished.

"Thanks. I used to cook a lot. Now I find the garden takes up most of my time. Do you want more pie?"

"Maybe in a minute." He leaned back in his chair and gave me an appraising look. "You said you needed sane company. For things in general or something specific?"

"Bit of both, I suppose. To tell you the truth, I was wondering if you knew anything about waste disposal companies."

If he thought this eccentric, he was too much of a gentleman to show it. "A little bit. I don't have a dump truck, so I used to deal with disposal companies when I was doing remodeling. Usual thing. Some reputable. A lot of sons of bitches."

"I'm afraid it's the latter I'm interested in."

"How so?"

I told him. More than I'd told Moira or the children or Herb or the detective. I suppose I told him because I didn't know him well, because he didn't ask me questions, because I didn't have any obligations there.

"I can't help you on the fellow with the tattoo. You know, haulers get a lot of transient workers—it's not the pleasantest job in the world."

"No."

"There's three or four big waste haulers in this part of the state—Tomco Brothers, Wehaul, and Waste Recovery Systems. What's more likely is that your truck was an out-of-state outfit or some real cowboy operation—unlicensed, the whole thing."

"Nonetheless, it might be possible to find out. If I'd only seen the plates."

"You should have reported it."

"The troopers weren't too impressed with our earlier experience."

Sam shrugged. "Perhaps because of your previous visits."

"That's it in a nutshell. They think I'm a crazy lady. Some days I think so too."

"Maybe you're like me and like to finish what you start?"

"That and wanting some explanations for the kids. Not for everything, but for a few things."

I was sitting on one of the high kitchen stools, and Sam got up and came around the counter and put his hand on my shoulder without saying anything. I understood then that he was lonely as well as kind, but instead of getting up and playing the hostess, I leaned my head against his chest. Outside the mower rose and fell, its full-throated roar tamed by the long slope down to the bottom of the garden. We were beginning to sell quite a few plants directly to the public, and Moira is big on presenting a good appearance. As a result, there was well over an acre to mow and the kids were on the last of it, working far enough from the house so that over the engine, I could hear Sam's heart. A strange heart. He ran his hand gently up and down my back. "Things will be all right," he said. I wondered if that were true. "You'll see."

The mower's engine rose to a crescendo, then whined and began to fade as Julie turned back toward the stone wall that marked the end of the lawn and the beginning of the pasture. I could feel Sam's thigh through my jeans, then he stepped in front of me, put his other arm around me and kissed me. I kissed him back. Why not? He seemed to know what he was doing, and he was just unfamiliar enough to erase disagreeable memories. I had, at one point in my marriage, tried lovers and infidelities. To get back at Max, to outdo him—whatever. But I couldn't sustain it, I was not cut out to live like Max, and I went to the opposite extreme—divorced him, joined a vaguely feminist commune, refused dates. But nature gets you in the end—your nature or Mother Nature or the nature of things—take your pick. After a month of disasters, I found myself entangled against the kitchen counter with Sam while the kids mowed the lawn outside. The kids!

"Sam, the kids."

"I still hear the mower." He kissed me again and continued his explorations. I was admiring the smooth hollows on either side of his rump and approaching the stage of dizzy acquiescence, when I was diverted by silence, by voices, by the sound of footsteps on the back porch. I sat up straight and Sam turned away and said, "I think I might have some more pie."

"We're out of gas, Mom."

"It's not dark yet. Do you and Julie want to get more?"

"I'll need money," she said.

I got down off the stool, feeling rumpled, and fetched a couple of singles. "Just to the station. That's all."

"Don't worry," she said, picking up the keys. "Oh, hi, Sam."

"Bye, Sam," said Doug. They went out, laughing.

"They seem to be doing all right," he said.

"Some of the time anyway. Better than their mom," I added ruefully.

"I didn't mean to start that," he said.

"Don't feel bad—I have a taste for that sort of adolescent love."

He laughed. "What we are reduced to by our children."

"Something like that. Unfortunately, there are too many

loose ends in my life at the moment." I was getting to sound like Moira.

"I'm getting over that stage," he said.

"How long does it take?"

"Couple of years."

"I'll have to keep having trouble with the sink in the meantime," I said. "To keep in touch."

"No problem having problems with your plumbing, Alice. Thanks for dinner. The sink's on me."

"I can't let you do that."

"I'll stop by for another piece of pie, then, and we'll call it even. You should sell pies, Alice."

"They're not as good for you as herbs and veggies."

"But better for the soul," he said.

$\triangledown$

Chapter 7

W E WERE ALL OUT the next afternoon: the kids were in school, Moira went off with some deliveries, and I took Skipper to the vet's for the multitude of shots deemed necessary for the modern house pet. While we were waiting for the needle, a smashed-up coonhound was brought in after a collision with a pickup, and it was close to four before we rolled into the drive, Skipper leaning out the window and slobbering with the relief and joy of being home. Then he started barking.

"Hey," I said, "that's enough."

Instead of settling down, he barked louder and bolted from the car the moment I opened the door. I took the groceries out of the trunk and followed him up the glass-littered walk: someone had smashed a pane in the old-fashioned door and opened the house. My heart jumped. "Doug! Julie!"

Silence. They would not be back from school. And Moira had planned to go straight to Todd's. I grabbed Skipper's collar and walked cautiously through the kitchen and dining room, listening for footsteps, breathing, the sound of an intruder—an intruder, perhaps, with a trucker's hat and an eagle tattoo. Nothing. The living room, too, was empty—emptier than usual, in fact, because the television set was missing, the disconnected cable wire limp on the floor like a dead snake. Damn! I let Skipper go and ran upstairs: Julie's stereo, Doug's camera, my computer printer were missing. The keyboard and monitor of my system had also been considered, for both had been disconnected and the diskette container tipped over in the process. I ruffled quickly through the disks for farm business, taxes, inventory, but they were not even out of order.

Back downstairs, I checked behind *Bullfinch's Mythology* for our bankbooks and safe-deposit key, which I found untouched. Amateurs, clearly. Some dirt-biker angry at being run off? A school feud? An out-of-work neighbor? I'd been foolish to be alarmed and began to feel angry. Then I noticed that the basement door was ajar and felt another twinge of fear: I dislike darkness and closed places even under the best conditions.

"Skipper!"

The old dog ambled over. Having raised the alarm, he clearly felt that his job was done. I took hold of his collar and opened the basement door. The cellar was very quiet, and I wondered if I ought to call the troopers. Then Skipper pricked up his ears and started for the steps. I switched on the light and, picking up a bottle left out for recycling, followed him into the low fieldstone basement, a massive, leaky structure inviting to wintering mice. As the house had once been coal-heated, there was a storage cellar off the main chamber, as well as a variety of closets and partitions. A row of barrels shielded one corner and old piles of firewood and bundles of rope and winter chains cast irregular shadows on the floor, longer than usual because one of the overhead bulbs had burned out. I could hear the irregular drip of water somewhere and smelled the earth and stone and mold and musty old timber smell of the house. Skipper stood with his head up and his thick tail stiff. "Go find him, boy," I whispered, and he bounded toward the coal cellar, sniffed at the base of the door, and barked.

"Who's there?" I called.

Silence.

I fought down an impulse to run up to the phone and

unlatched the door. It swung open and Skipper pushed past
me to lunge at something in the corner. I heard a squeal,
then the dog's excited bark: a mouse, perhaps a rat. I was
laughing with relief when the sound of breaking glass came
from the kitchen. I dropped the bottle and ran to the stairs.
Another crack, then the metallic tinkle of glass on cement.
I took the steps two at a time and saw Doug silhouetted
against the bright afternoon light. "I see you broke some
glass," he said. "I almost cut my hand getting the door
open."

"Careful with taking that out. And get the trash can or
Skipper'll cut his feet. Someone broke into the house."

"Into our house?"

"Only one around. Where's Julie?"

"She's looking at the goats."

"I'm afraid they got her stereo."

"Julie!" he called, excited to be the bearer of bad news,
"Julie!"

I dialed the troopers' barracks, while Julie stormed in and
Doug discovered the loss of his camera. "Stupid thing was
broken anyway!" I heard him say.

"Well, isn't that goddamn lucky!" Julie said. "I've lost my
stereo."

"Nothing too serious," I told the officer. "My daughter's
stereo, my computer printer—smallish things. They un-
hooked the rest of the computer, then decided against it."

"Probably kids. Maybe an addict."

"Maybe," I agreed.

That was still the verdict when they came out: a pleasant
round-faced fellow with too much belly and a sunburned
nose and Detective Crombie, looking as spiffy and efficient
as ever. I was surprised to see him. "I thought they reserved
you for capital crimes."

"Oh, I thought I'd take a look. Under the circumstances."

"I don't think there are any circumstances," I said. "Whoever did it smashed the back door window and scooped up
what could be carried." That's what I hoped, anyway. Odd
how our minds work. I'd been quite prepared to take our

poacher seriously—and quite put out when the detective didn't. The truck likewise. But I didn't want anything close to home to be serious. We'd had our share, so to speak; we'd paid our dues already with Max.

Crombie gave his professional smile and said he'd like to have a look around. "Have you touched anything?"

"Well, the glass in the back door. And a box of disks that had been knocked over."

"Who else uses the computer?"

"Moira and I do business records on it."

"Moira?"

"My business partner, Moira Perez. And Doug and Julie use it for homework, term papers, that sort of thing."

"Any trouble with the neighbors?"

"None I can think of. I did discourage some kids on dirt bikes from using the pasture. They were frightening the goats. But that was quite amicable—they didn't know we had livestock. Deer hunter last fall—same thing."

"You teach, Mrs. Bertram. Is that right?"

"Yes, but we're pretty far from the U Branch. I can't think of a student who'd have this energetic a dislike. Classes are over, grades have been out for a couple of weeks—it's a bit late in the day."

"You brought me a disk," he said. "A computer disk like these."

"Exactly like. Max used the same type of system."

"Did you bring me all you found?"

"Of course. And if I find more, I'll certainly inform you."

"You're still looking?"

"Why not?"

"You just don't seem to be lucky, Mrs. Bertram," he said mildly.

Julie said something similar later, when she was still bemoaning the loss of her stereo.

"You'll just have to save up from your job at the store," I said. "Once school's out, you'll earn enough."

"Couldn't you loan me—I'd pay you back over the summer."

"Dear, I can't do it. I don't know how we'll replace the printer as it is—and we need that for our billing."

"None of this shit would have happened if we'd stayed with Daddy," she said.

"Perhaps not. But I couldn't stay with your father. And I'm not sure staying together suited him, either."

"You always said that, but I know he didn't want the goddamn divorce. He told me so."

"No," I said, beginning to get angry, "he wanted to go on the way he was, regardless of what it did to the rest of us."

"The rest of us were happy," Julie said. "You never consulted the rest of us."

There was some truth in that.

"And look what it did to him. Look what happened!"

"You can't blame me for that—whatever it was. All right, I couldn't live with Max. I'd loved him and he was driving me crazy. He was a good father but a lousy husband, and if I'd stayed with him—"

"You'd have fucking killed him," Julie said. And then she went quite white; she'd said too much, gone too far. Of course, she'd been in the house that day—the day I'd picked up the .22.

"Don't be bitchier than you have to be. You could have gone to live with your Dad and Bev, if—" But I bit my tongue. I wouldn't say that Max had been quite content to be a weekend father, to be free.

"I could have been killed and I wish I had been," she said, bursting into tears.

"Stop that!" I tried to put my arms around her, but she began struggling wildly and caught me in the mouth with one elbow. I hit her in the face with my open hand, and there was a brief, humiliating struggle before she broke free. "I'm getting out," she said. "I'm not staying here." She eluded my grasp and ran to the stairs.

I touched my pocket to make sure I had the car keys, took a deep breath, and followed her out to the barn, where I found her crying beside the car. "Nothing can bring him back, sweetheart," I said. "Nothing can change us. We have to live with that." When she didn't answer, I put my hand on her shoulder for a moment. Then I returned to the house, though my impulse was the same as hers—to get into the car and drive somewhere else and find someone else's problems. Sam's, maybe. At the moment, I thought maybe Sam's might be nice.

The next morning we made the papers again, the nearest town being small enough so that a village robbery was reportable news. At lunchtime, Professor Friedland phoned. "Alice? What's going on out your way?"

"Damned if I know, Ted. No real harm done, though."

"Glad to hear it. Listen, I saw the story this morning and thought about you and your article. Can you come over to the lab?"

I hesitated a moment. This was the busy season and I hated to take up more of Friedland's time on a fishing expedition. If I did, I'd pretty much be committed to produce something.

"I wanted Doreen Hale to contact you," he continued. "It really is her data, but she called in sick this morning."

Doreen Hale's data was another matter. "That's kind of you, Ted. I think I can manage. Is two o'clock all right?"

"Fine," he said. "Fine. At the lab. Third floor of Grindle."

I thanked him, got through my share of the garden in good time, and appeared at the double glass doors of the lab at two o'clock sharp. Friedland was beaming.

"Good to see you, Alice. Good to see you." He motioned me into the lab, a tall, bare room with gray lab tables and several thousand miles of glass tubing. A couple of white-coated students were at work and Ted introduced them, pointing out the type of analysis each was doing. I made suitably impressed noises.

"The public," Ted Friedland said, "really doesn't know what's involved in pure water."

"No, but that may be just as well—on a daily basis."

"Quite the opposite. Eternal vigilance is the price of a glass of water—and the avoidance of hepatitis, cholera, typhoid, and genetic damage, just to mention a few of the possibilities. Water companies, of course, are required by law to test their own supplies for both organic and inorganic compounds, including herbicides, pesticides, known carcinogens, and for bacteria counts. There's hundreds of known contaminants and the labs do a good job, but that doesn't touch the rivers and streams not tapped for drinking or private wells and springs. We do random well samples and we're trying to look at the water supply as a whole."

"Doreen said you were building up a data base."

"That's right. Looking at good natural resources and their degradation. Yes, her thesis material has been most useful. And because of our sampling program around the state, we hope to function as an early warning system for water resources." He nodded. "We're useful but not immediately useful. That's been our problem. The trustees, the legislature—everyone wants short-term results, immediate action."

I remembered that the Water Resources Lab had had its funding cut, and Friedland's solicitude began to seem practical. "But now you have something immediate?" I asked.

"I wouldn't normally go right to the press with this, but you can hint in an article," he said.

"Possibly. Hint what?"

"You spoke to Doreen about her data."

"Yes. I was interested in the river—local fishing, swimming—a natural for the paper."

"Right. And she told you it was in pretty good shape."

"I was glad to hear it. There've been all sorts of stories about rural dumping. And big trucks have been seen in the Mashantucket."

"She raised the dumping issue after your conversation. We have you to thank, Alice. We decided to run a couple more tests. Something's going on, but it's not ordinary toxic dumping. The river's too clean."

"What else would be worth the trouble?"

"Red-bag waste."

"Sounds bad. What's that?"

"Medical wastes, needles, syringes, blood samples, body

parts, radioactive wastes and isotopes. Doreen detected some radioactivity in one of her samples—very slight, you understand. It was just luck it was picked up. I don't want you panicking the public with a 'hot river' story."

"And you think it came from a medical waste shipment?"

"Almost certainly. It's not industrial stuff. That's the good news."

"You mentioned needles, syringes—the stuff that's been washing up on beaches?"

"That's right. Fortunately, not ours—yet. New York and New Jersey have suffered losses in the millions from their tourist trade. In terms of overall pollution, it's trivial stuff and almost certainly harmless, you understand, but highly sensitive politically. Mama finds a needle at the beach, she sees her kid getting AIDS. And aesthetically—"

"I can see that. Especially with body parts. But would it be worthwhile to truck this red-bag stuff all the way to the Mashantucket? I mean for whoever's dumping it?"

"Very. Medical waste is beginning to be regulated and it's expensive to process—you're not just supposed to stash it in a landfill. There are a number of companies now that specialize in red-bag collection and disposal. It can be a very lucrative business, especially if they're charging top dollar and then chucking it in a river somewhere."

"I see. You mentioned some companies that specialize—any in this state?"

"As a matter of fact, there are two, United Biologicals and Bedford-Martin. Both divisions of big and supposedly reputable firms."

"Supposedly?"

"We've just had an early warning that someone is taking the cheap route to waste disposal. Maybe some rogue outfit. Maybe not."

"Well!"

"Handle it discreetly, Alice. Maybe 'University Water Resources laboratory head predicts that the Connecticut shore will be the next to suffer from the plague of medical wastes.' "

Ted had obviously been rehearsing.

" 'Some of the Thames system shows evidence of medical isotope contamination. This presence is very slight and completely harmless, but detectable by the advanced equipment at the University's Water Resources Laboratory.' Something along those lines. We don't want to panic the public, just alert them."

"And send a message to the legislature at the same time?"

He smiled. "It can't do us any harm."

I was on my way back home when I remembered that we were nearly out of stamps, so I swung by our former post office. Thanks to Max's voluminous correspondence and his enormous number of newspaper, magazine, and journal subscriptions, I had been a steady customer, and Eunice, the postmistress, recognized me at once.

"Mrs. Bertram! Good to see you. Have you moved back into town?"

"No. Just visiting. I was over at the University."

"Well, how nice. We miss you—and Professor Bertram," she added. "I don't know what to say—we all felt terrible."

"Thanks. That's kind, Eunice." I felt myself smiling awkwardly and said, "Let me have two hundred first-class stamps, please."

"We all liked him," Eunice continued as she reached into her desk to show me the current variety of commemoratives. "Don't you believe about him acting strange! Cheerful too. He came in with your daughter just a few days before. What a fine-looking girl! What beautiful black curly hair—she'll get that from you, I imagine, but darker. How old is she now?"

I kept my face still: Julie is browny blonde and bleaches lighter. "Julie's sixteen."

"I'd have guessed seventeen or eighteen, though she's very dainty. They grow up fast nowadays."

I agreed with that.

"She was helping the professor, carrying a bunch of packages and envelopes."

"Was she?" I signed my check and passed it over. "My

contribution to the postal deficit. Thanks a lot, Eunice."

"You're very welcome," she said, turning to a customer who had just come in. "And say hello to that girl of yours. So pretty and friendly."

A pretty, dark-haired girl young enough to be Max's daughter! I didn't like the sound of that, though perhaps she was another graduate student. I'd ask Stella. Or the pleasant Ms. Ryan. Or maybe I'd decide I had enough on my plate and forget Max altogether. That would have been the smart choice.

$\triangledown$

Chapter 8

T HE BIG, BLACK MERCEDES filled the driveway, emphatic as an exclamation point. I pulled the Honda over onto the grass and got out. From the back of the house, I could hear Doug's voice and the hard leathery sound of a baseball striking a padded glove. When I came around the corner, I saw him playing catch with Herb Rosen. Herb had taken off his suitcoat and rolled up his white shirt, and he was throwing high in the sunlit air so that Doug could practice fly balls.

"Hi, Mom!"

"Hi, dear. Hi, Herb."

"Business calls, Doug," Herb said.

"One more, one more to show Mom."

Herb goodnaturedly whipped the ball in a high curving arc down the lawn. Doug raced after it, turned, backpedaled, realized he'd misjudged the distance, and lunged again, scooping the ball up just a foot from the ground. Herb applauded. "Way to stay with it!"

Doug trotted up, beaming. Herb took off the glove and handed it to him. "You'll be ready for the team. You go to high school next year?"

"Maybe I'll make the JV's," Doug said.

"I should think so. You've got to work on keeping your eye

on the ball. It's not size, it's not even speed that's important most of the time, it's knowing where the ball is."

Doug nodded solemnly, and Herb laid one hand affectionately on his shoulder. "You practice some by yourself now. I need to speak to your mom."

"Sure, Herb, thanks," he said, but I could see how reluctant he was to leave: he missed Max, missed having a man around in a house full of women.

"You're good with kids, Herb."

"He's a fine boy. I've been remiss in not coming before."

"You've got plenty of your own to worry about."

"This is different." His face was serious. "I owe it to Max. You and me, Alice, we're not *sympatico*, are we. Why's that?"

Herb was rarely reflective, and for once, I tried to be serious with him. "Just in the nature of things, I guess. You and Max were best friends. As I recall, you didn't really approve of me."

"I didn't think Max would be happy with you."

"Well, I guess you were right about that."

"No, I was wrong," Herb said. He avoided my eyes and watched Doug throwing the ball. It rose tiny in the sky, then lost itself against the apple trees before disappearing into his glove. He turned and waved, and Herb gave him the thumbs-up sign. "Max needed stability in his life, and you provided that. Without that—"

"I couldn't be Max's keeper forever," I said. There was a subtle undercurrent of blame in all this talk about my virtues.

"No, you'd put up with more than your share," Herb said quickly. "But I feel an obligation. I feel a duty here, Alice. Though you don't want it, I feel that."

"Come see Doug now and again, if you like. He needs male company."

"A difficult age," Herb said. He put his arms behind his back like Prince Philip and started toward the house.

"I'm looking for one that isn't difficult."

"You're always so cynical, Alice."

"Yeah, I guess I am."

Herb reached into his coat pocket and pulled out an envelope. "I was sorry to read about the robbery."

"What's this?"

"To replace your stuff."

"Herb, thanks, but I can't take this. Our insurance—"

"They'll discount your deductible and take off for age and before you know it, you'll get enough for a nice Italian dinner. Take this and pay me back with what you get from the insurance, if you want. I'll be angry if you don't."

"All right. That's very kind of you, Herb."

"I owe, Alice. I owe it to Max."

We shook hands. He got into his big car, tooted the horn at Doug, and rolled down the drive. As I waived good-bye to him, I guessed that I'd misjudged Herb: he was a good guy who'd been trying to be kind.

The phone rang just after supper, and Julie, who was expecting a call from the stables, jumped up and answered. "Hello," she said. I was scraping the plates for Doug, who was doing the honors at the sink, and it was half a minute before I realized that Julie was uncharacteristically silent. I glanced over and saw that her face was white, her eyes round with shock.

"What's wrong?"

She was shaking her head back and forth, and when I reached for the phone, she was holding it so tightly I couldn't take it from her.

"Julie!" I leaned closer and then I heard the voice, hoarse, obscene, at once desperate and dangerous: ". . . owes me, you stupid cunt. He killed my kid. Don't think I'll forget that. Don't think it, you fucking bitch . . ." He was swearing and crying, terribly drunk, and this time I didn't try to reason with Warren Landis, I just reached over and cut off the call.

I put my arm around Julie. "It's okay," I said. "It's okay. Bev's husband goes off now and then. He doesn't know what he's saying. It's okay." But I didn't feel okay and neither did Julie. I made her sit down and told Doug to pour her a cup of coffee.

"He's called before?" Her nervousness with the phone suddenly made sense.

She nodded.

"Why didn't you tell me? It's since I went to see him that day, isn't it? Damn it! I should have left well enough alone. How often?"

She was crying softly. "A couple of times."

"We'll get the number changed. Leave it unlisted." Though I could see difficulties with that. "Maybe have a work phone that we put on the answering machine at night. He calls in the evening?"

"Or late afternoon."

The bastard!

"The other times weren't as bad. He just asked for you and mumbled."

"We'll get the phone company onto it. And the police too, if he calls again. He's upset, you know. He blames me. He blames us all for surviving." I hugged her again without getting much response. "Tell me if there's anything else. Phone calls, anything. You let me know, all right? Just hang up and let me know."

We talked about that for a while, and although Julie settled down, in some ways I felt worse. I wanted to ask Doug about the car he'd seen parked down our road the other day, but I didn't dare raise the anxiety level any further, and I was going to bed before I remembered he'd said it was a big, dark Taurus wagon. A Taurus was okay. Warren Landis's vehicles encompassed a variety of makes, but nothing new, dark, or distinctive. I told myself that it was important to keep down the paranoia and went sensibly to bed.

Warren Landis's call did have one result. Even though I was obligated to Ted Friedland, I don't think I'd have pursued United Biologicals if it hadn't been for his call. Landis was a trucker, UB trucked waste. Waste had been detected in the riverbed of the Mashantucket where Max had been hiking, cheating on Bev Landis. It made a kind of emotional sense that fit with a murder survivor's apprehensions. I called both the firms Fred had mentioned, saying I needed information for a story. I wasn't able to contact the PR person at Bedford-Martin immediately, but UB, their competitor, invited me for the next day and I decided to go.

I'm not sure what I'd expected from United Biologicals—perhaps a sleazy old warehouse in a dubious section of town. I was certainly not expecting the gleaming corporate fortress, formidable as a medieval stronghold, that was set off I-84 among similar palaces of business and industry. The type was characterized by an abundance of sheer concrete and metal facets, cantilevered overhangs, smoked, impenetrable windows, and a general air of arrogance and paranoia, as if, even in these pseudo-sylvan surroundings, replete with corporate ponds and woods, there was a fear of invasion, violation. Security was omnipresent, from the graffiti-proof walls to the floodlit parking lots to the uniformed guard, stationed behind an expanse of polished travertine and potted plants, who checked my name and identification against her list of expected visitors.

"You'll need a badge," she said, handing me a piece of plastic laminate. "If you'll have a seat, we'll call Mr. Williams."

I thanked her and sat down in one of the handsome leather and chrome chairs. My badge identified me and announced that I was allowed "limited access." Across the lobby, workers were arriving in a steady stream. They wore their badges clipped to their shirts or belts, and entered in twos and threes, some with Styrofoam cups steaming in their hands. There were no other visitors.

"Mrs. Bertram!" He'd been to the same school as Detective Crombie, though he was as short and heavy as the detective was tall and trim. He had the same air of pleased surprise and professional friendliness, the same warm handshake, the same cautious eyes.

"How do you do, Mr. Williams. How kind of you to see me."

"Always glad to help writers." He knew me as a freelance writer, which was no lie. I'd done a good deal of journalism while the children were small and still wrote occasionally, though now usually in the winter season when the garden is dormant. "I thought I'd show you the building and give you some general information about the United Biologicals story. We have some printed matter—writers always seem to like that."

"Easier to be accurate," I said.

"Without a doubt. And we appreciate accuracy. Like all new companies, we're trying to present our image to the public." He shook his head as if the burden of UB's image weighed on him personally.

"You are a new company? How many years old?"

"Well, new and old. Originally, we were a biological-supply firm—the tapeworm you dissected in high school probably came from the old Biological."

"Ah," I said. "There's an interesting fact. Could you find out for me how many worms you produce a year for biology classes?"

"Probably can. Then we got into medical supplies, principally laboratory equipment and so on. This, by the way, is the employee cafeteria," he said, pointing through a bank of glass doors. "Along the way, we got involved in the disposal of radioactive materials. We had been handling small amounts of radioactive isotopes—for cancer treatment—and had to develop procedures. I can arrange for you to talk with Doug Murator about that, if you're interested—it's a specialty in and of itself. We've acted as consultants for a number of clean-up jobs, most notably the Kelly Company's old New York warehouse. I don't know if you remember—it was an old radium storehouse. Toxic as hell. So we'd had some experience in hazardous material. Then hepatitis B. In here is our main computer area—tracking shipments, billing, inventory. A monster number cruncher."

I made appropriate noises, before asking the relevance of hepatitis B.

"Hepatitis B is generally passed by infected blood or contaminated needles or surgical implements. Since there is no known cure, the spread of hepatitis B has meant new safety precautions for medical staff. In fact, a medical worker is many times more likely to be endangered by hepatitis B than by AIDS. But the HIV virus has turned out to be the driving force behind a whole new phase of waste disposal. The growth in red-bag waste has been enormous. And the concern behind it is AIDS."

"It's an ill wind," I said irreverently.

"You said it. Do you know how much infectious waste is generated a year? Five hundred thousands pounds. It has to go somewhere. And it's due to increase as we increase the numbers of disposable hospital products. Some predict medical infectious waste will double every year for the next ten."

"Though there is some debate about what should be classified as hazardous, isn't there?"

"UB is going with the Centers for Disease Control on that one," Williams said with a superior air. "They've recommended caution in handling anything that has been in patient contact—bandages, packing, needles, blood and body parts, of course—the gamut."

"Opportunity for your company," I agreed.

"Indeed. The thing is, this stuff just doesn't go away. Take a hospital. It's supposed to either autoclave or incinerate all infectious waste."

"Autoclave?"

"The waste is processed in a sealed chamber by steam under pressure."

I dutifully wrote this down. I was actually planning an article, but possibly not what UB had in mind.

"So they autoclave it or incinerate it—you've still got the ash, which has to go to some hazardous waste landfill. And that means proper handling on the way."

"Which means your company again."

"Right."

"Which must mean trucks and things," I said. We had reached the top floor now and were facing the executive suites. The building was designed so that these ran along a balcony overlooking an atrium filled with flawless begonias and cinerarias, backed by glossy banks of succulents and ivies. Once we had our greenhouse, there was a market for corporate greenery that Moira and I had not considered.

"Our own fleet," he said. "I'll get some printed matter for you. The whole UB story."

I looked out to the vast parking lot and the band of woods beyond. "Not here, surely."

He looked surprised. "What's not here?"

"Your trucks."

"No, no, this is strictly corporate offices."

"And where do you keep your trucks—the nuts and bolts of the operation, so to speak?"

"Well, it's complicated," he said, showing no inclination to enlighten me.

"In what way?"

"Well, naturally UB has its own fleet. But the way the business has expanded, we've had to subcontract some pick-ups."

"And disposals?" I asked.

"Never disposals," he said firmly. "You understand that in a number of states, including this one, hospital waste is tracked from cradle to grave. It's important for you to be accurate about that in any story. UB tracks every piece."

"How do you manage it?"

"A paper trail—like bills of lading. No, no, disposal is in UB's hands."

"And would I be able to arrange a visit to your garage? Photos, you know, trucks rolling in and out, carrying toxic waste to the latest in disposal—you know the sort of thing."

"All visits to the East Hartford base must be cleared higher up."

"Perhaps I could check."

"You understand, security is a prime concern," he said, glancing at his watch. "That is really all I can tell you. You'd have to apply again through the central office. Unfortunately, I have another appointment in a few minutes. Suppose I take you down to Doug Murator's office and let him fill you in on our disposal of radioactive waste."

Seeing I would get no further with him, I said that would be fine. Mr. Murator proved no more informative about what I really wanted to know than the PR maven, and by ten-thirty

I was crawling through the Hartford construction traffic toward East Hartford. Two and a half hours later, having traversed most of that sprawling suburb without coming up with UB's garage, I pulled into our drive, just behind Sam's van.

"I was passing," he said.

"Glad to see you anytime. What about pie and coffee?"

"The magic words," he said.

"Actually, you're the man I want to see."

"Oh?"

I unlocked the back door and hung up my purse.

"You're looking pretty sharp today."

"Thanks. I was out interviewing at UB—sorry, United Biologicals. An infectious and toxic waste handler that Doreen mentioned Max was interested in."

"Any luck?"

"Well, yes and no. They apparently have a fleet of trucks and also sublet some of their pickups—but no disposals. That was a sore topic."

"But you're dubious?"

"I wanted to see the trucks—picture opportunity, you know. But, no, all I was told was that the garage was in East Hartford."

"No sweat."

"Hah! That's what you think. I've been all through that wretched burg without a hope. Even called the police. Nothing listed under UB."

"You just don't know where to look," Sam said with the satisfied air of inside knowledge.

"And you do?"

"I told you, I used to deal with waste haulers. I've a pretty good idea where most of the garages and warehouses are."

I put a piece of pie down on the table for him. "Coffee will be ready in a minute. Let me get a piece of paper and my map, then you can tell me where to go."

"I have a better idea," Sam said.

"What's that?"

"Come out some night for an early dinner with me and we'll track them down."

"At night?"

"When you saw the truck, wasn't it?"

"Yes, and early evening they might be loading. That's a good idea, but I'm not sure you want to get involved."

"Why not let me be the judge of that. And dinner? Is that a good idea too?"

"Yes," I said. "That may be the best idea you've had."

Chapter 9

W E HAD A CURRY at an early-opening Indian restaurant, an unpretentious eatery where our slacks and sneakers were not out of place. We did not talk about UB and its trucks, nor about other topics of obsessive interest. Instead, we talked about gardens, about the best varieties of early corn, about what would be easily managed plantings for the front of his house, about the company he used to own, the colleges we'd attended, his time in the military. Sam was good company. The best thing was that he'd only known me post-Max and so did not bring with him the luggage of my awkward spouse, my smooth-seeming but actually disastrous marriage. Just, I suppose, as I knew nothing of Laura, his wife. I was customer Alice with a set of wonky pipes. He was Sam the plumber and might have been dropped from Mars. I found both attractive.

"Not much here in the dessert line," he said when the various vindaloos, rices, and breads had been cleared away.

"Then let's skip dessert. What time is it?"

"Six-fifteen. A good hour and a half, two hours till full dark."

"But you know where we're going."

"You'll see," he said.

Outside, we got into his pickup. Sam had insisted on

driving and insisted on his truck, which was a solid, heavy machine with a manual shift more responsive than my automatic Chevy. A half dozen miles down the highway, we circled off an exit ramp to a residential area of aluminum-sided homes and small, neatly mowed yards. I had checked this same street but had given up too soon. Not far from where I'd turned back, we merged with a major road and entered a steel and concrete zone of industrial concerns, garages, and warehouses, floodlit, cyclone-fenced, guarded. The sidewalks were empty, the wide, divided street relatively quiet, and except for a few hardy weeds, the area seemed as bare of vegetation as a mountain on the moon.

"Bravo," I said. "But which one?"

"That I don't know. There are quite a few truck depots and loading areas. Keep your eyes open for any markings."

"Wait! Can you stop?" I asked a moment later.

"Damn, I have a car right behind us. I'll have to double back. A UB truck?"

"No, Tomco Trucking. That was their garage. Their owners are cousins or something."

"Cousins of?"

"The UB owners. Same family, different branches."

"No wonder they don't want visitors around the trucks and garages! Tomco's been a mob outfit for years."

"You're sure about that?"

"Ask anyone in the business. They've got the garbage hauling sewed up in some of these towns. You know, commercial waste. They haul in New York and New Jersey too."

"The industries there haven't the savoriest reputations."

"No, indeed." He turned around at a cross point in the center divider and started back. "Which one?"

"The brown roofs up ahead. I saw the sign. I think there's a side street."

"Yeah, I see it." Sam pulled across the traffic and got onto an access road that passed several warehouses, garages, and businesses before disappearing beyond the line of street-lights into a scrubby wasteland. Sam drove by the Tomco establishment twice. It consisted of two large corrugated-

steel garages and a series of sheds. In the back were several
large dumpsters and an assortment of barrels, the whole
well-fenced, with a guardhouse at the main gate. There were
quite a number of large, rather dirty looking dump trucks,
garbage compactors, and containers but nothing that connected with clean and glossy United Biologicals. "Too bad
you didn't get that truck's license," Sam said.

"They look the same type. Big enough, certainly." I took
my binoculars out of the case and said, "Let's park at the
side, so we can see what's going on."

"You don't want to try to talk our way in?"

"Not tonight. They'd be more apt to recognize the truck
later."

"Want me to write down the plate numbers?"

"Please. I can read them off through the glass." Not much
was moving at the garage, and the few trucks about the yard
were soon cataloged. I rolled up my sleeve and checked my
watch. It was after seven. "Maybe I was wrong," I said.
"Nothing much doing."

"Wait a bit, then if we don't see anything, let's go and ask
for someone. Say he works for UB or something."

"All right." I smiled at Sam and returned to the binoculars.
At one end of the long garage, an overhead door went up. I
could see two men in coveralls, one with a trucker's hat.
They went into the garage bay together, one emerging a moment later. His walk seemed familiar, but that was perhaps
my imagination.

"Put away the binoculars," Sam said. "I think we've at-
tracted attention."

I was lowering the glass when I saw it: a small, clean truck
with the same steel blue and white that had decorated the
UB publicity handouts. "Sam!"

He reached for the binoculars. "Under the seat, the case,
too!"

Over his shoulder, I saw a burly man approaching. He
wore brown coveralls with Tomco Trucking stitched onto a
patch over his breast pocket. "Let's go," I told Sam.

"No need to make them suspicious," he said. He opened

the door of the pickup and leaned out. "Can you tell us how to get back onto I-84? We've gotten turned around somehow."

We got a sullen look. "Nowhere near 84 here," he said.

"We were afraid of that. We'd decided to try 44 east," Sam confided, "but there's too much slow local traffic. We've been going around in circles trying to get back on the highway."

"Get off this street. It's strictly for access. Go east on the boulevard into the center of town. You'll see I-84 signs there."

"Thanks a lot." Sam shut the door and started the motor. Our adviser stood on the sidewalk and watched until we turned into the traffic.

"There was a van there that I'm sure was from UB. Do you think there's a back way into that street?"

"Maybe. We'll try another of the access roads. I used to get plumbing fixtures from them," he said, pointing to a showroom cum warehouse. "Let's try this one."

The floodlights were coming on, big cold eyes hanging off the edges of windowless buildings or perched at the top of thin steel poles, each circled with a cloud of moths. We drove past the fenced buildings and out into the glass-studded waste of subsoil and weeds that rings industrial areas. Sam found a dirt track that petered out at a mess of rubbish, and he reversed the pickup and returned to the road. The next entrance led to a construction site; Sam hesitated. "Probably guarded," he said.

"Maybe something farther on?"

"We'll see. We can come back here, if we don't have any luck."

Just before the paved road ended at an orange and white crash barrier, Sam spotted a gravel track that, though rutted and full of rocks, wound down one small steep hill and up another to reach the street where Tomco was located. We parked beside a restaurant supply shop and walked to a row of Tomco containers that were lined up along the fence. For a moment, I didn't see anything, then I saw the neat little UB van. It was parked right in the open bay, and men in

gloves and coveralls were unloading bundles from the back.
I handed the glass to Sam.

"All red," he said. "Like the bags that fit commercial floor
sanders."

"That's medical waste, I'm sure. And I don't think UB's
going to dispose of it legally, no matter what their PR says.
Can you see what they're doing with it?"

"No. But maybe into a larger truck."

"I'd like to be sure." Faintly over the murmur of traffic on
the boulevard we heard a door slamming. The UB vehicle
started across the lot toward the exit. Sam and I waited by
the fence, occasionally looking over our shoulders, but apparently only vehicles raised the alarm: who, after all, goes
walking in these urban deserts? About ten minutes later, we
heard a heavier engine start up in the garage and ran back
to where we'd parked. "Watch which way he goes," Sam said.
"I don't want to get too close right away."

A large brown truck pulled out. Once on the boulevard, it
lumbered as far as the crosspoint before signaling a left turn.
"He's heading east," I said.

"That suits us fine," said Sam. "Just try not to lose him
before the highway."

Not much was doing in the center of town, and although
a few cars cut in and out in front of us, we had no trouble
keeping the Tomco truck in sight. A few miles down the road,
it slowed under an overpass aswirl with starlings and took
I-84 eastbound. Up on the interstate there was enough traffic to keep us from looking obvious, and Sam turned on the
radio, Mozart first, then, as the signal faded, a rock and roll
station playing oldies, The Doors, the Everly Brothers, Don
Maclean's "American Pie": echoes of a personal history now
as remote as the pharaohs. The sky was darkening, the little
lights and dials of the cab glowed in the blackness, and two
cars ahead, the Tomco truck rode, big as a bus.

Sometimes, when I was still married to Max, I would see
someone passing in a car and try to imagine myself as that
person. I would visualize the road unfolding ahead and feel
for a moment what it would be like to be in that car, holding

that wheel, headed for whatever destination my imagination could conjure. That was how I'd tested the limits of escape and the sensation of difference.

Mick Jagger was painting it black in a voice stolen from the delta, when Sam said, "Funny, how you remember this stuff." He meant the music—and other things.

"I find I don't learn new songs anymore. I don't even hear them, though the kids have their music on loud enough."

"It's maybe only important for a few years unless you're a musician."

"A few years of susceptibility?"

"I guess. A susceptibility to music and—I don't know."

"Love," I said. "Fool love. You're susceptible for a time and then you spend your declining years getting over and tidying up."

"I suppose it's knowing the susceptible period," he said. "Knowing when it ends and when you're safe."

This was an uncomfortable topic, and in self-defense I watched the roadside zipping by, the sharply lit exit lane, the neat grass and trimmed highway shrubs against the amorphous black jumble of woodland. Then I felt the truck slow; we were nearing the end of the superhighway, where the road narrowed and divided. Sam dropped behind a station wagon until he could see where the truck intended to go.

"Of course, he won't signal," I said.

"Be hard to lose him anyway. Aha, you're right so far," Sam said as the truck kept east. "He's going the right way."

I watched the red lights at the back. I might be right. And about Max? All this was tangential to Max and whatever had happened in the cottage. It was one more little piece, one more indication that Max had had something more on his mind than his latest conquest, that my original impulse had been correct.

At the second town we passed, the station wagon pulled off onto a side road, leaving us and Tomco. Sam was not thrilled, although it was not unusual to be followed by a car or truck for miles along this route.

"We'll pick up some traffic on the bypass," I said.

"He'll be getting a good look at us, that's all."

"None of this was quite real before," I said.

"That truck has a high degree of reality. But we're not going to be able to follow him all the way."

Neither of us had planned this far. Finding the warehouse had been the thing. "If he goes to the forest, we'll see where he turns in. I know a lot of places to stop."

Sam, no doubt thinking about his truck, was noncommittal, but before we had a chance to decide on a course of action, the Tomco driver surprised us by leaving the bypass ramp, not north toward the Mashantucket and the river, but south.

"Oh, shit," Sam said and changed lanes abruptly. Tomco drove down a hill toward town, then turned left without signaling. Sam followed onto a narrow road that sprouted branches in a half dozen directions, all quiet, dark, and without traffic.

"I think there's a trailer park up this way," I said.

"Some old industrial works too. But I'm afraid we're going to be pretty obvious."

Tomco turned again, so abruptly that Sam had to slam on the brakes; this time we did not follow. Instead, Sam drove on a quarter of a mile, turned around in a driveway, and started back.

"Think that will fool him?"

Sam shrugged. "Which one did he take?"

The heavy foliage made it hard to tell one opening from another. "This one," I said. "No, no, I'm wrong. Take the next one. Opposite those mailboxes."

Sam slowed down and turned into a narrow, green tunnel. The truck lights reflected off a tangle of trees and shrubs growing so near the pavement that it was impossible to see around corners. Sam slowed down, then realizing that the road went for quite a distance, speeded up. "We may have lost him. Holler if you see any kind of cutoff."

"I don't think there's anything," I said. "Maybe I was wrong about which road he took." Just then, we rose a foot in our seats and jolted all our vertebrae on the return drop.

Sam hit the brakes, the truck's shocks groaned, and our lights bounced up and down before a solid wall of trees and the muddy patch of earth where the paved track had ended without warning.

Sam opened his door and stepped out. "Hard left," he said. "Though it's not paved."

Outside the peepers were singing, loud even over the sound of the engine. "Any sign of them?"

"Looks like it. We can turn here okay, if we can get out of this mud."

Sam climbed back in and put the truck carefully into reverse. The wheels slid and caught, then ground with a high whine. Sam shifted into first, but though the truck rolled forward obligingly, once reversed it settled back into the mud like a hog at a wallow.

"Do you have a board or anything we could put under the wheel?"

Sam got out without answering. I heard him walk around to check the wheel, then open the back of the pickup. I leaned out the window. "Any luck?"

"No. There's a flash in the glove compartment. Get it, will you? Maybe we can find a log that will do. Shut off the engine too," he said, as I started to climb out. "This is a good light."

I turned the key and automatically stuck it in my pocket. Sam was crunching through the weeds and brush at the edge of the track. "Hold this a minute," he said, handing out a heavy strip of bark. "Might do."

I threw it on the ground beside the wheel. In a few minutes, we'd found enough small logs, sticks, and bark to cover the mud, and we were laying them in place when we heard a car on the side road.

"Better move," Sam said. We jammed the bark under the wheel and kicked a final log into the mud.

"We may need something under the other wheel," I said, but the lights already sweeping through the trees swung round to blind us—high lights, a small truck or a big off-road vehicle that was coming too fast for the track and too fast for the surprise of a truck across the road in the darkness. Its brakes locked, the vehicle slewed left, right. There were shouts, followed by a roar of sound that rattled along the truck body and told me that Sam and I might well meet the same fate as Max, Beverly, and Timmy. "Run," I said, and lunged toward the trees. The lights canted at a crazy angle, a branch cracked overhead, and Sam came thrashing through the brush after me. Behind us were shouts, another shot—I gave a name to the sound then—and ignoring mosquitoes, ticks, and snakes, I scrambled over a fallen log and dropped flat on the ground. Sam had had a similar inspiration, and we lay panting with nerves and sudden exertion, aware that the wood around us had gone quiet, that even the peepers were holding their breath.

Two men were on the road, one with a light. We could hear their voices, a profane mixture of exasperation and anger. Then we heard the rustle of branches being pushed aside, the sound of twigs snapping. They were coming into the wood, not directly at us, but to one side, panning the light across the ground and up and down the trees. My immediate impulse was to run, but it was too late. Sam and I pressed our heads to the leaves and mud and stopped breathing. The beam of the flashlight glittered on the branches over our heads like a thousand fireflies, then passed on. The man nearest us began swearing: he'd floundered into some water and was sure there'd be snakes. We could hear his thrashing and the steadier tramp of his companion. Surely they'd turn around soon, and when they did, Sam and I would be pinned against the log. We started to wriggle backward, discovering as we did a multitude of jagged branches. Sam had squeezed himself out of sight when one gouged a line across my back and caught my shirt. I reached frantically to untangle the fabric and heard the searchers stop. Expecting the light, the voices, the sound of a shot, I flattened myself against the acid smell of the leaves, but instead there was a rumble on the road, the high whine of hydraulic brakes, shouted orders. "Just a fucking minute," someone shouted not fifty feet away and began running heavily toward the road.

A noisy conference ensued between the newly arrived truck crew, who wanted "to get the hell outa here" and the two men who'd been preoccupied with us. I heard the metallic clink of a truck hood being lifted; a moment later, Sam's pride and joy sputtered to life. I took advantage of this to disengage myself, and Sam and I retreated farther into the trees. From the road, we heard shouted directions, the whine of wheels, then the purr of the engine as the tires found purchase on the logs. The truck was backed up and driven off to the left, followed by the off-road vehicle. The Tomco truck pulled out a moment later, its lights passing overhead, whitening the branches.

"We'd better get out of here," I whispered. "They'll maybe come back."

"I'm not leaving without my truck," Sam said.

So we waited. The peepers started up again, and battalions of mosquitoes swarmed around our heads. I was ready to run all the way to the highway to escape them, when we heard a motor: it was the same high, off-road vehicle.

"They can't have gone far," I said.

"Right," Sam said. "Let's go." But though we headed toward the road, we were unable to retrace our steps in the darkness and found ourselves in a little bog. Sam splashed into a shallow pool with enough noise to freeze us both in our tracks, but besides the peepers, the only sounds were from the mosquitoes, which seemed driven to frenzy by the prospect of our escape. I could feel them biting through my shirt, even through my jeans. I touched Sam's arm and he stepped back onto the mossy bank, which now and again slid away to wet places that sucked around our ankles. Cold, muddy water was seeping into my shoes, and I knew that we'd walked farther than we should have. "Which way, do you think?"

We both stopped, then Sam took a step forward and reached back to draw me after him. Through the branches we could see a pair of round bright lights. A hundred yards farther on, we reached the edge of a clearing. The swampy woodlot, which extended back to the road in one direction, had been cut in a circle around a large building—a shed stretched to three or four stories—with a huge door opening nearly the full height of the front. The works had originally been for casting concrete pipe, apparently, for in front of us were a number of enormous culverts and drains, and we left the buggy shelter of the trees and crouched behind them. Sam's truck was parked in the open doorway, almost concealed by the blinding glare of the floodlights that cast a sour, orange tinge over the yard. From our new vantage point, I could just make out the outlines of what might be machines or scaffolding or some sort of hoist. There was a battered-looking gray and red car parked to one side; otherwise, no signs of life.

"Did you see how many were in the truck?"

"No," Sam said, "but I'll bet they've left someone. They'll figure that sooner or later we'll come for the truck."

"Or walk out to the road," I said. "They can't watch everywhere."

"They could leave someone on the road—I think there's only one way out."

"We could maybe get closer," I said. "See if we can spot anything."

"Pretty hard with that light."

"We'll have to go back into the wood," I said. And though neither of us was keen on the noise and the discomfort, it was getting late and we resigned ourselves to beating our way though the brush. A quarter of an hour later, we pushed through a clump of sumac and found ourselves at the top of a bare sand, stone, and gravel bank. "Shit!"

"Building's in shadow anyway. They didn't bother to light the back."

"I suppose we can get down further around," I said and started to stand up.

"Careful," Sam whispered. "There's someone."

He had just stepped around the side of the building with a nasty looking gun and a flashlight. We ducked as he directed the beam up the hill, probing the bushes. Then he lowered the light and walked slowly around the back, stopping now and again to run the light over the trees. When he disappeared around the far side, I looked at Sam. "What do you think?"

"Let's wait and see if he comes out again. We don't know where he is in the building."

"There was a bright light to the right of the door," I remembered. "Maybe an office."

"We'll still need to move to where we can make a run for it," Sam said, but that did not prove easy to do. It took us quite a while to work our way off the gravel bank and down to a tangle of brambles, weeds, and large rocks near the back of the building. Stiff from crouching, we straightened our backs and were just about to leave our shelter, when we heard a tuneless whistling. The man walked over toward the gravel bank, his flashlight a bright cone, and urinated against the sand. Then he returned to the building without bothering to walk all the way around. Sam held up the fingers of both hands, then pointed to his watch, and I nodded. The second indicator on the dial crept across in slow red flashes, one number changed, another. I became aware of an odd smell, a disagreeable, perfumey, chemical odor, at once sharp and cloying, somewhere between lavatory cleanser and roach spray, which had laid an oily breath on the night air.

When it was time, I asked Sam if he wanted the truck key but he shook his head. We stood up and stepped from cover, everything dark and still behind us, the floodlit yard ahead as bright as a ball field. We crept over the hard-packed dirt and crumbling asphalt, bits of broken glass crunching eerily under our feet. Twice we stopped, sure we'd been discovered, but as we came to the corner of the building, we heard the one-sided sound of a telephone conversation. Our man was mostly listening. "Yeah," we heard. "Yeah, okay." The big shed door framed Sam's truck. But though both of us were tempted, a square of yellow light revealed the office, where a man in coveralls was sitting talking on the phone. We dropped into a crouch and scuttled into a dimness full of tanks, huge funnels, and block and tackle rigs on triumphal-

arch-sized trusses. We slipped behind the supports of one of
the lifting rigs and waited until our eyes adjusted to the
backlit dazzle.

A sound, steps, and the office door opened. He knew we
were there. That's what we both thought when the man
stood silhouetted against the gray-orange ground, a curtain
of dust and moths caught in the spray of light. He didn't say
anything, just stepped forward and switched on the overhead
lights. We could see everything: the huge rivets and bolts
holding the trusses, the smears of rust on the vats, the cob-
webs, the man's big frame, his thin, sharp face with a sheen
of sweat on his forehead, the black outline of his weapon.
He sensed that we were there and he had only to step forward
a dozen paces to see us, but he wasn't sure. Perhaps he was
a coward. Perhaps his orders were ambiguous. When he took
a step, I forced myself not to look at his face, not to stir his
nerves with even unseen eyes, and in looking away I saw the
gray fuse box like the one we'd installed when the cottage's
ancient wiring had been redone. Four feet, five feet away. One
good step evened everything out. I touched Sam's arm and
moved my head a fraction of an inch. Sam's eyes left the
man—who had stopped and turned toward the wall. I saw
Sam take a breath, then he nodded. There were footsteps at
the front of the garage, the sound of a doorknob, the click as
the office door closed again, the faint sounds of a phone being
dialed. Sam and I stood up together. I tried to open the box
gently, but the catch was stiff and Sam had to take out his
pocketknife. There was a slight ping as the metal cover
swung open. I touched the master switch, hoping it would
cut the floodlights as well, then looked back: my route lay
around the vertical parts of the lifting device, past three
tanks or molds, and over some debris to the truck.

"Let me get to the office door," Sam whispered. "I'll stop
our friend." I looked at Sam, taller than I but slight, however
tough, and the thought came to me that maybe Max wasn't
worth this. I put my hand on his arm, but he shook his head.

"No other way," he said, and stepped around the girders
toward the door.

I closed my fingers around the switch. Sam's shadow leapt back at me like a goblin. When he reached the door, he glanced back and nodded and I pulled the switch.

The darkness was startling; blinding black velvet swirled with auras of red and green like a cheap painting. I heard a shout, footsteps, reached out to the girder, turned around it, bashing my shin on one of the vats: how many?—one, two, the third one was farther apart—I hadn't noticed. Distracted by the sound of the door, I practically fell over some wood, then heard a blow and the heavy wood and metal thump of a weapon on cement. I could see the outline of the truck, darker against the thinning darkness of the night sky, and I scrambled to the door and jerked it open. The light went on, as startling as the darkness, and I heard a shout. The key was in my jeans pocket. I stuck it in the ignition and fumbled the gears, forgetting momentarily that this was a manual drive, before the engine came to life. I shifted into reverse, edged back, then pulled on the lights, which turned the inside of the shed a golden yellow, flashed black with shadows. There was a figure in the mirror, dark behind me, holding a rifle. I thought disaster and stepped on the gas, but as the truck jounced over the sill, Sam slapped the side and yelled for me to stop. I stabbed the brake, stalling the motor. He jerked open the door, stuck the rifle behind the seat and said, "Let's go! He'd been calling someone."

"Are you all right?"

"You're forgetting my time in the army," Sam said.

The truck lights raked over a figure lying prone in the doorway. "Is he all right?"

"Wind knocked out of him," Sam said. "Better shift it into second. You're straining the engine."

"Could you tell who he was calling?" I asked when we reached the street.

"Police, I think," Sam said, quite unconcerned. "I think that's a siren. Stop and I'll get rid of this." He lifted the rifle from the back.

I braked, shaking the truck back on its haunches. "Better let me drive," Sam said. He opened the door, jumped out, then took the rifle by the muzzle and flung it into the trees. I slid over, and Sam got in and put the truck in gear. We could hear the siren weaving toward us through the maze of little streets.

"We don't want to meet them," I said.

Sam seemed not only untroubled but semi-euphoric. Men, even the nicest of them, are the fanciful sex: the creators of the most pernicious romances, the wildest myths.

"The trailer park," I said. "Next road."

He turned down a row of immobilized mobile homes, pulled smartly next to one that was all dark, cut the lights, and shut off the engine. The sirens, two police cars, passed up the road toward the works. My heart jumped. I'm basically conservative, law abiding, unfanciful. We heard them returning twenty minutes later. They went by without a glance. "You're a bright lady, Alice," Sam said. He gave them another quarter of an hour then started for home.

"I'm afraid this has gotten you involved," I said when he turned into my driveway.

"We'll take the offensive," he said. "Call the troopers about the dumping. Place, date, truck number."

"Right. But there's your window." The windshield had a neat round hole with a ray of cracks spreading across one corner.

"It's usable."

"I'm sorry anyway. I appreciated your coming."

He shut off the motor and turned toward me. The porch light illuminated the lower half of his face, leaving his eyes in shadow. "When I'm with you," he said, "I find myself doing surprising things."

"Is that good?"

He seemed to be considering. Then he leaned over and kissed me. He smelled of mud, leaves, and sweat, and I put my arms around him and felt his back, long and supple, his wiry strength. When he drew away, I asked if this was one of the surprising things.

"Yes. I'd kind of lost interest, you know."

I did know. "It happens."

"The kids are home?" It was really more statement than question.

Funny how interest comes and goes. "Yes," I said and took a breath and added, "afternoons. They're not home sometimes till four-thirty. Swimming and Julie's horse and—"

I could see his smile hanging in the half-dark like the Cheshire Cat's. "Afternoons I'm sometimes free," he said.

$\triangledown$

Chapter 10

T HE SKY WAS STILL pink when I woke up, threw on a t-shirt
and jeans, and went downstairs. Skipper's heavy tail slapped
the floor in greeting, and the cat began howling to be let in.
The wooden porch was cool and damp under my bare feet,
the grass beneath the oak tree webbed with a dew already
vanishing in the early sun. Beyond the pasture, the sky
turned gold and set a few scrappy gray-blue clouds floating
after a pair of geese. I could hear a thrush, robins, the mimic
mew of a catbird: this was the best time of the day, the best
part of country life. When we'd been a commune, I'd been
up every day at dawn. I am not really a communal person,
and dawn had offered solitude and a chance to get things
done before the inevitable debates and discussions of group
living.

The cat began rubbing insistently against my legs, crying
plaintively, and I went inside to feed her and Skipper. Then,
without waiting for the coffee, I pulled on my rubber work
boots and went out to the garden. We'd had a load of manure
delivered when the ground was too soft for the truck to drive
up to the new beds. That meant a fine pile to shift, and before
the flies came out was the best time to do it. I fetched the
barrow and a pitchfork, chalking up another little lesson for

the novice entrepreneur: order manure while the ground is frozen. Put it on the calendar.

Around seven, I heard Julie's alarm clock ring and straightened my back and stood for a moment, leaning against the fork. Another hour of work at least, maybe more. I'd finish up, I thought, and let Moira do today's weeding and transplanting. I threw the pitchfork on top of the load, lifted the smooth, dirty handles, and steered the wheelbarrow over the soft ground. It wallowed in and out of mole damage, stuck on an inconvenient clump of weeds, had to be muscled around a rock too big to be pried out of the earth. I saw movement in the house, a light in the bathroom, then Doug's torso, clad in white t-shirt and briefs, passed his open window. He was slight like Max, short like me. Were things going all right for him? Julie had wept and shouted, run wild with the Russell boy, and thrown up a load of beer on the back porch, but she seemed to be coping now. She was more grown up, a little more thoughtful, a little less demanding: she might turn out to be a good person. Her behavior was uncouth, but her instincts were sound, and lately I'd seen that she had more staying power and common sense than I'd expected. She'd be all right. But Doug, so good, so quiet and manly at the funeral—I wasn't sure about him anymore.

"Mom! You want coffee?"

"Please. I'll be right in." I jerked the barrow over a soft, deep rut and tipped the manure onto the ground. I stuck the fork into the pile and looked at my watch. I'd been working for an hour and a half, had most of the pile moved, and felt not tired but hungry: to tell you the truth, pound for pound I'm as strong as anyone around. Thanks in part to Max, I've found the life that suits me best.

Sam called just as I was saying good-bye to the kids. Our adventure had left us both a bit high, and we exchanged small talk and agreed that we were two terrific investigators. Then he said that he'd have the plumbing roughed in for Morris Digby's new bathroom by Thursday morning, leav-

ing him pretty much free Friday afternoon. Although it was
unlikely that I'd forget, I marked this on my calendar.

I was feeling optimistic, in spite of a persistent hooting in
our phone that the company assured me could not be
checked before the end of the week, in spite of missing a call
from Chet Wolfe, a reporter who was one of Max's old
friends, and in spite of a stack of bills and correspondence
that occupied me for most of the afternoon and well into the
evening. It was by way of relief from these chores that I
reopened Max's account of the Salisburys. The manuscript
was much enlivened by long extracts from their letters, and
I was browsing through difficult deliveries, an influenza ep-
idemic, and post–Civil War mansion construction when I
became aware that the screams, sirens, and rock of the kids'
rented horror video were reaching a crescendo. A moment
later, Doug came up and hung around my door, neither in
nor out. He does that when he wants to talk about something, but I was too preoccupied to make the connection.
"How was the video?"

"Kinda gross."

"Yeah?"

"Killer vultures."

"Not very accurate."

"No, but there was this guy . . ." He gave me a synopsis
heavy on special effects and violent deaths.

"You'd better go to bed," I said when he was finished. "If
your homework's done."

"It's done. I told you that."

"I thought you had a quiz."

"Not on Friday." He drew out the syllables in irritation,
and I thought about Sam and wondered if I'd go, if I wanted
to go. If I wanted involvement. "You are my own dear and
my best friend," one Salisbury had written to his wife.
"Though we have had twenty years together, it seems no
more than as many weeks. And if we have twice as long again
together, it will still not be enough." This after they had lost
one farm and three children and moved on to Ohio to start
over. I wondered if they made marriages like that anymore.

"And school," I asked Doug, "is school all right?"

"School's boring," he said and went abruptly to his room.

To tell you the truth, I was worried about him and about school, which I feared had become an ordeal. I should have probed more, but I had too many worries—the kids, the farm, the bills, the whole mess of Max. If bright spots like the dumpers' arrests or Sam came along, I tended to concentrate on them, and I wasn't thinking about Doug at all when the phone rang Friday lunchtime. I'd finished my coffee and was putting my feet into a pair of loafers. I had a decent shirt on and my best slacks. It was one-thirty; the car keys were in my pocket, and I was due at Sam's in ten minutes. Though I was tempted to go out the door and let the answering machine handle the vinyl-siding offer, the improved credit card, the worthy cause, I lifted the receiver.

"Mrs. Bertram?"

"Speaking."

"Mrs. Bertram, this is Lydia Kane. I have Doug in my office. I think you'd better come down to school."

Her words sank into the pit of my stomach and tightened up the back of my throat. I'd been expecting this, I realized. "What happened? Is Doug all right?"

"There was a fight. Doug's shaken up, but he wasn't hurt. I'll explain the whole situation when you get to school."

"I'll be right over," I said. The keys were in my pocket, my heart was in my mouth. I ran to the car and pulled out in a spray of gravel. On the way to school, I alternately blamed Max and myself, Max for the whole mess and myself for ignoring the cues, for an absorption in what had happened to the neglect, perhaps, of what was happening. I rolled through a stop sign at the highway junction and had to slam on the brakes when peripheral vision picked up a tanker truck. Down the highway, over the side road. The school was fairly new, set like a corporate headquarters in a clearing in the woods. Students were playing softball on the diamond as I passed; a big blonde girl swung at a pitch, a thin boy in the outfield slapped his glove, a crow stalked the edge of the field, looking for Fritos and cookie crumbs. I parked next to the building and went down the long tiled corridor to the office. The band was practicing in the auditorium with a heavy thumping cadence that matched my heart. I stood among the tardy, delinquent, and supplicant in the main office until I caught the secretary's eye. "Alice Bertram," I said. "I got a call from Dr. Kane."

"Come around this way." I followed her to the principal's office. Doug was sitting on one of the straight chairs, holding a wad of Kleenex. His face was swollen, and he had the beginnings of a bruise under one eye. "Dear, what happened?" I stepped forward to put my arm around him. He felt stiff and hot, and I noticed that there was blood on the front of his shirt. I looked at Dr. Kane, who was standing behind her desk. "There's blood," I said.

"The other student's been taken to the hospital," she said. "I'm afraid this is a serious matter."

"Who?" I asked.

"Peter Cardine."

"The big kid?" I asked Doug. The Cardine I remembered was a swaggering bully who'd given Doug trouble his first year in the school.

He nodded without speaking, and I patted him on the shoulder and sat down next to him. "Maybe you'd better tell me what this is about," I said, looking between him and Dr. Kane.

"Doug has not been too responsive," she said. "I've spoken to Bill Grange, our industrial arts teacher."

"This happened in shop? What the hell were they doing?"

"It was just at the bell," she said quickly. "They were apparently putting equipment away."

"He said I was crazy," Doug said. The words came out in a rush, a gulp of air. "Crazy like my old man."

"Not the first time," I suggested.

He shook his head.

"I was afraid of this," I told Dr. Kane. "You will remember that I discussed just this possibility with you and with Doug's and Julie's counselors."

"Mrs. Bertram, we've done our best."

I had my doubts, but I said, "I'm not blaming anyone. So what happened? Looks like you got punched."

"The fucking idiot punched me," my son said, his face flushed with rage. "I hit him back. He's always hitting me. I hit him back. I told Granger that."

"He was holding a hammer," Dr. Kane said. "It looks as if the Cardine boy has a broken nose, possibly a broken bone in the face."

I could hear the sound, the scuffle, the mix of casual cruelty and anger, then the soft thump of metal hitting bone and flesh. I felt sick, but I said, "He hit you first?"

"He's been picking on me for weeks, ever since—"

"But he hit you first?"

He nodded.

"Maybe you'd better let me talk to Dr. Kane for a few minutes." I looked at her over my shoulder and she nodded.

"Doug can go and sit in the nurse's office," she said. "She'll put some ice on that eye."

"A bit late in the day," I said. I was upset and frightened for Doug, who had been saddled with my temper.

"You understand the first thing was to separate them and see to the Cardine boy. He could have lost an eye or—" She shrugged, unwilling to contemplate the further reaches of disaster. "They may sue you."

"Their kid's a bully twice Doug's size. If they have anything to say, they can speak to my lawyer."

"He was attacked with a *hammer*, Mrs. Bertram."

I was aware of that, but I decided to take the offensive. "A school hammer. In a supervised class. I don't think I'd encourage the Cardines, if I were you."

"Certainly not. But this is serious. As for Doug—"

"How big a hammer?" I asked. I could see from her expression that Dr. Kane had no idea they came in different sizes.

"A hammer," she said. "Just a hammer."

"It does make a difference. With a sledgehammer, Cardine is dead. With a tack hammer, he has a bruise on his face. I suggest you find out right away."

She thought that over, and I did my best to look in control.
Dear God! What was I going to do with Doug? Counseling?
A different school? She picked up the phone and asked Bill
Grange to come into the office. I knew him a little, because
he was one of Doug's favorite teachers, and I hoped I
wouldn't have to make trouble for him. He came in a moment later, a tall, heavy man with a blond crewcut—the last
in the county, I'd guess. He came over and shook my hand.
"Not like Doug at all," he said.

"A lot of strain," I said. "And a bit of harassment, I'd
guess."

"Yeah, there's always a few," he said. "Not in class, but
once out of sight . . . They were in the equipment locker at
the back of the shop. I was checking that the saws were—"

"Mrs. Bertram asked about the size of the hammer," Dr.
Kane interrupted. She was thinking suits and investigations
and impassioned letters to the press.

"It was a little ball-peen hammer. Not a big head." He
held his fingers an inch and a half apart. "Enough to do
damage, though. I really don't think Doug even knew it was
in his hand. Apparently there was some pushing and shov-
ing—some bad feelings—and that was it. He took a swing."

"Out of character," I said.

"Very much so, though he's had a hard time lately."

"He's seen his counselor," Dr. Kane said.

Neither Bill Grange nor I said anything to that.

"He'll have to be suspended. For an attack on another
student."

"Even in self-defense?" I asked.

"No more than a week. I'll talk to the students who were
there," Dr. Kane said. "Maybe three days."

I sensed that this was her best offer. "Maybe a talk with
the Cardine kid too," I said. "And if you could suggest someone for Doug to talk with."

There was some discussion about this and another talk
with Doug. By the time we were back in the corridor, heading
for the door, my legs felt shaky. Doug had said nothing to Dr.
Kane, to Bill Grange, or to me. We got in the car, fastened

our belts. His cheek was still red, but the ice seemed to have helped the swelling. I touched his shoulder. "It'll be all right," I said. "Sounds as if he deserved it. But you've got my temper. You'll have to watch that."

He gave me a curiously opaque look, as if he were remembering. Well, let him. At the last moment, I hadn't. I'd gotten under control. "I want to go home," he said.

Near the general store, I asked if he was hungry, and since I didn't feel like cooking, we stopped and bought grinders for dinner. It was getting on to five when we got home, and we were finishing dinner before maternal anxiety lifted enough for me to remember Sam. While the kids ate ice cream sandwiches, I went into the office, closed the door, and dialed. Sam listened to my rather incoherent account—problems for the kids get me a lot more upset than Max, the Salisburys, the Tomcarellis, and their cousins the Forgettes, all together. Then there was silence.

"I'm sorry," I said.

"Were you really coming?" he asked.

Then it was my turn, but I didn't have to hesitate. "I had the car keys in my hand," I said.

Chapter 11

Monday I was gratified to see a little story about arrests for illegal dumping at the former Konkret Kast Company. The toxins unloaded were apparently gaudy enough to have interested the writer in the company, and, though short, the article included a couple paragraphs about Tomco Trucking. Tomco's dubious services were described as "absolutely vital" by a number of elected officials from our smaller municipalities, and its principal owners, Bobby Tomcarelli and his wife, Suzi, were characterized as "socially prominent patrons and philanthropists." I knew for a fact that they were bastions of the opera company and heavyweight contributors to the symphony and ballet. They were also politically significant, and, in an odd coincidence, the Salisbury name surfaced in passing. I suddenly had the feeling that had Max completed his manuscript it might have been pretty interesting. I chewed this over while I cleaned up the breakfast dishes.

Doug, in official disgrace, went out to help Moira with some potting while I conducted negotiations with a couple of restaurants. After that, the three of us set out young tomatoes and peppers, then busied ourselves assembling the wire cages that we hoped would protect the harvest from blemishes and slugs. We had a late lunch, Moira requisitioned the truck so that she could take one of her young goats to the vet, and I jammed the little Honda with flats of lettuce for a garden center near campus. For service rendered, Doug was allowed out to visit his friend Mike Pasolini and headed off with Skipper as I drove away. "I may be late," I called to him. "I have to pick up a textbook on campus."

He smiled and waved, a slight boy in jeans and a t-shirt, the big golden dog beside him. That's what I thought of first, when I saw what had happened: Doug and the dog and the hilly country road stretching open and lonely in both directions.

But when I got back around five, I wasn't thinking of danger and isolation, I was thinking about the text I'd picked up: whether it was enough of an improvement to merit new preparation for me and increased costs for the students, whether I really preferred *Othello* to *Hamlet* and *The Wild Duck* to *A Doll's House*. I was thinking about those things and I had put the car in park and shut off the engine before I felt that something was wrong. I stepped out of the car. The kitchen window was broken, and I was aware of flies and a smell. As I ran to the house, I yelled for Doug, for Julie and Moira. The back door had been stove in and, inside, everything smashed or overturned: pictures torn from the walls, china broken, books thrown about. I climbed the stairs, slipping and sliding on papers, on bits of china and glass, and went frantically from room to room. I threw open the trap to the attic, hesitated in terror behind the closed bathroom door and the closets, then ran down to the basement, calling, imploring. Nothing. In the shambles of the kitchen, I stood still and told myself that Julie was at the stable, that Doug was at Mike's house: I'd mentioned that I'd probably be late.

My heart began to decelerate. Out the window, I now saw raw earth, tire tracks, a swash of broken plants, ruts, twisted metal, and smashed coldframes. A surge of nausea broke against the back of my throat: two, almost three years' work—not all gone, surely! I ran outside: someone had driven a truck through the gardens, once, twice—mashing the young lettuce and herbs, uprooting tomatoes and peppers, and grinding the strawberries into mud. One-third, one-half, maybe more, of our stock was gone, already rotting—and there was a smell in the air; I'd sensed it first. That's how I'd known to run to the house, why I'd feared—I heard a cry, agonized and uncomprehending, and ran blindly toward the barn, thinking of the children, of Moira, of Max and Beverly and Timmy. There were big black flies around the goats' pen and the gate was open. I let out a cry when I saw them, then the smell of blood hit me.

They'd killed the goats. With a knife and the sledge that stood in the barn for driving stakes and fence posts. Killed them cruelly, smashing their thin legs, their long, alert faces, their coolly skeptical eyes. As I stepped into the shed, a kid struggled to its feet and lunged frantically away, dragging one shattered leg behind it. Another goat seemed stunned, but not badly hurt, and when I touched her back and legs, she seemed to know me, although she couldn't stop trembling. The others, six of Moira's milkers and two kids, lay dead in a mess of blood and dung. The kid with the broken leg might or might not survive. I stood up, my hands red, and called the adult goat out into the sunshine, away from the horrors that had been its companions. The wounded kid hid in a corner. Afraid of frightening and possibly injuring it further, I left the shed door open and went to call 911, the stable, Mike's house, and the vet. Then I went back out, drew some clean water for the two surviving goats, and managed to get the injured kid wrapped up in a blanket. I left them cowering in the outdoor pen and went to assess the damage to the gardens.

The ruts were a foot deep where we'd mounded up the soil; a big truck, a dump truck maybe. I thought of that later, of the possibility of determining the type of tire, of tracing the truck through that and soil traces, of all the paraphernalia of detection. At the moment, I went about picking up support wires, righting coldframes, digging salvageable plants out of their premature graves. A section of thyme was muddy and trampled but no worse. The mint, virtually indestructible, was unsalable but still vigorous, the newest lot of parsley was gone, but the oregano had survived and one row in five of sage. The newly set-out tomatoes, raised in our now-ruined plastic shelter, were a loss, though there were a few flats intact, and I started on them, picking up those that had been kicked aside rather than overturned and culling the broken plants. I went through the beds, frantically, irrationally, absorbed in anger and sorrow—and relief too, for Julie had been kept late at the stable, and Doug and Mike were still out on the Pasolinis' pond in the canoe. It could have been them, I thought, as I worked, picking plants out of the muck, cleaning up, putting right. It could have been them. My shirt was stained with dirt and blood, my sneakers were coated with mud. And before? Could that have been what happened? Was this what Max had come back to find? Was that the story? I could not think, could not imagine. I was on the remains of the peppers before I heard the siren, the cars, and I could not stop, could not straighten up until I heard the voice for the third time and looked up to see Detective Crombie.

"It could have been the children," I said. "They're all dead but two."

"Maybe you'd better sit down," he said.

There was a hose pipe near where he was standing. He turned it on and I put my hands under the stream of water.

"Was anyone hurt?" he asked.

"The goats. They killed the goats." I gestured toward the pen. One of the troopers was walking toward the fence, panicking the two surviving animals. "Wait," I called. "Wait for Moira. She's on her way. They're terrified."

"Better check the house," Crombie told the trooper, who had stopped uncertainly at the gate.

"Dead animals in the shed," he said.

"How many?" the detective asked.

"Eight. Killed with a knife and a sledgehammer. The barn was always open." I was shaking uncontrollably.

"There's blood on your jeans," Crombie observed. His voice was careful, neutral.

"I'm covered in it. They'd both been hurt." Then, belatedly, I realized the import of his comment. "One has a broken leg. The surviving nanny has superficial cuts. I brought them outside, away from—"

"I see," he said. "And your children?"

"Not home, thank God. Julie's at the riding stable—the Havens' place—and Doug had gone down to Mike's, the Pasolinis, third house on Morgan Road. With the pond," I added foolishly. "They were on the pond when I called."

"You called them?"

"Yes. I was afraid for them. When I came home, I mean. When I saw that the house had been broken into."

"And you called right away?"

"No, not right away. I went through the house, through the garden and the barn. Then I called you and the children and the vet—Moira was at the vet's."

"When did you leave?"

"I don't know. Two-thirty, three. Moira may know. She went out just ahead of me—one of the goats had gotten cut on some barbed wire. Bit of an infection. Doug was home from school—he was walking down to Mike's as I was leaving. He'll know the time. He remembers anything with numbers," I added. Detective Crombie wrote all this down in his little black notebook. I could see the notebook and his hand moving, writing, and his dark shirt behind it and a white square of the house behind that but nothing else. The earth, the plants, the strip of lawn, the roof of the house, the angle of the shed had been obliterated. I'd lost my peripheral vision and I felt on the verge of losing the rest. "I think I'd better sit down," I told him.

He put his hand out and grabbed my arm and walked me over to the lawn, where I sat down and put my head against my knees. The world swirled dark around me like a picture losing focus and the sound of the truck and Moira's voice were far away. I heard the pain and got up. "I'd better tell her," I said, forgetting I'd already told the vet—who was there, too, a stout youngish woman with short dark hair, saying, "This one's in shock," and taking out her kit.

"What the hell happened?" Moira asked, her voice shaking.

"Someone wrecked the place. Drove a truck through the plants, busted up the house."

"It's too much, Alice. It's too goddamned much!"

"We'll have to get a statement," Detective Crombie said.

"You'll damn well have to wait. That's Dickins," she said to the vet. "I'll get hold of him."

"Leg looks bad."

"He's the best of the lot. Try to save him." Tears were running down her face, and I turned away toward the house.

"She's acting like she blames you," Crombie remarked. "Why is that?"

I turned to look at him: neat and spiffy, no mud on his boots. "She might better blame you. How many times did I go to see you? Call you? The house was broken into—wasn't that hint enough?"

"Now just a minute, Mrs. Bertram. You have pursued a case that was officially closed. That is your business. It is not necessarily our business. Your obsession with your ex-husband's death raises a lot of questions."

"So does your refusal to see what's in front of your face. You've got truck tracks a mile wide. Those don't belong to any vehicle I'd have access to—nor vandals, kids, whatever the excuse is. Dump truck, I'd guess. Like the one down at the Konkret Kast plant—and the ones along the river."

I could see the wheels turning. "You didn't call," he said.

"I was afraid you wouldn't take me seriously."

"Any other ideas?"

"Warren Landis. Bev's husband. I don't like to think so, but maybe. He called a couple of times with drunken threats and scared my daughter half to death, but I didn't think it would come to anything. We changed our phone number and that seemed to discourage him."

There was the sound of a bicycle on the gravel drive, then Doug's voice. "Mom! What's happened!" I stepped past the detective and ran down the drive. "You've got blood on you," my son said.

"The goats. Someone hurt the goats."

"Not Peter," he said. "It wasn't him, was it?"

"I don't think so," I said, but, of course, all this had to be repeated for Detective Crombie. When he finally went inside to examine the rest of the damage, I got permission to pick Julie up at the stable. "I'd appreciate it if we could get the goats moved, covered, whatever," I said, "before Julie gets home."

Moira said she'd call Jack Mawson at the next farm. He had a little bulldozer and might be willing to scoop out a grave for us. I touched Moira's shoulder and took out my car keys.

"They believe you now?" she asked.

"God knows. The detective went on about 'my obsession with the case.' But that was before he looked at the tire marks."

"You do look a bit—" she gestured toward my blood-smeared clothes.

"Moira, I'm so sorry. I couldn't do a thing for the others. Just got them out of the shed and put a blanket on the worst one. The rest were—"

"I know," she said kindly.

"It could have been Doug or Julie," I said.

"I think chez Todd," she said. "For all of us. His house is enormous."

I stood still and looked around. The pen was empty; the vet had gone with the two injured animals. The gardens were a shambles. The house needed setting to rights. Then I shook my head. "I'm not leaving," I said. "But if you could take Doug and Julie for a few days—"

"As long as you want, but—"

"Someone has to stay, and it should be me. It's my fault that I never know when to give up."

The police left in the dark, packing away their photos and their samples, their measurements and their notes. Jack Mawson's bulldozer had scooped out a trench behind the corn patch, and Moira's pretty goats were covered with a layer of earth and lime. Doug and Julie had been packed up, protesting, and Todd himself had arrived in his big Lincoln to take them and Moira downstate; Detective Crombie had approved of this move. Somewhere between the garden and the goats he'd gotten serious, and Doug's report of a strange car hanging around was given a good deal more importance than our earlier experience in the forest. Daisy Mawson brought over some macaroni and cheese, and pitched in to help tidy the worst of the kitchen. She wanted me to go back to the farm with them for the night, but Skipper, smelling death and missing Doug, was so uneasy and restless that I thought I'd better stay with him. I tied him up outside and sat down to a plate of warmed-up macaroni. Just as I was finishing, a truck pulled into the yard.

I sat motionless at the table and felt adrenaline mingling with panic: I was getting skittish about trucks. Skipper barked once, twice, and I had time to regret leaving him tied up before there were steps, a knock. I saw the shape against the light, the long barrel, and threw open the door.

"I brought you this," Sam said, handing me a .22. "I think you mentioned you can shoot."

"Come in, Sam. You must be a mind reader."

"Moira called. I came by twice, but the Smokies were still here. I thought I wouldn't complicate things more than necessary." He looked around the kitchen. "Looks like a tornado. Any plumbing damage?"

"They went for the cash crops, I'm afraid. We're ruined but civilized—the fixtures are intact."

He leaned the rifle against the counter and handed me the clip. I examined the metal square reflectively and gingerly picked up the .22.

"It won't bite," he said.

"I used to be quite a good shot," I said, but put the weapon down quickly. "What about some coffee? And there's some pudding left."

"Let's see," he said, opening the refrigerator. "Rice pudding! One of my favorites."

"Have it. I may be peddling it along the roadside in a few weeks."

"Are things really that bad?"

"Well, that will depend on the insurance. We'd already

sold off much of our potted stock, but I'd say ninety percent of what was left is destroyed. Our plastic shelter is repairable, but the flats inside are almost all ruined. We'd just set out tomatoes for a crop—they're gone and the supports ruined. Peppers too. Strawberry bed salvageable but no crop to sell. Herbs ditto. Moira's goats are a loss plus vet's bills, though if Dickins can be saved, he's an asset. That's assuming she wants to keep on. Of course, we'll be way behind by the time everything's cleaned up, and I'm supposed to be buying out her share of the house. That's impossible now, I'm afraid."

"Moira will wait."

"Maybe, I don't know." I felt like crying and looked away. In the dining room, some of my mother-in-law's china still littered the table. Two nice prints were scratched under their shattered frames. I went in and picked up the shards of china, then began to knock the jagged pieces of glass out of the frames. Sam brought in a wastebasket and we worked in silence for a time.

"How about upstairs?"

"Not so bad. Books and papers thrown about."

"A quick job."

"Yeah. I suppose they didn't want to be caught."

"Pretty stupid, nonetheless."

"Or completely reckless. We were lucky no one was home. It could have been the children—or Moira."

Sam thought about this for a time. "I could do with a drink," he said.

"I drank up the gin with the murders. Cheap red wine is all."

"Better than nothing," Sam said philosophically. "You look exhausted. Sit down."

I righted a couple of lamps and sat on the couch in the living room. Books that had been tumbled out of the tall cases drifted along the floor. The remaining picture tilted off its hook at a forty-five-degree angle, but I'd lost my compulsion to straighten and tidy. We were sitting on some sort of psychological faultline, and I'd never keep up.

Sam brought the wine bottle and the two juice glasses. The California red was coarse and strong, and I drank it like medicine.

"Why do you think it happened?" he asked after a time.

"They were trying to scare us. Maybe looking for something too."

"Must have been."

"But I don't know what they were after. Max knew about the dumping, I'm sure of that. He'd been along the river and he knew Doreen's work. But if he knew something more, he took it with him or hid it too well."

"Maybe it's something they only think you have."

"That's almost worse," I said. "I can't give up and hand it over."

"But you wouldn't do that anyway, would you? I can tell."

I shrugged.

"I want to know why."

"You've asked the hard one," I said. The wine was coming down like a woolly hat, like a second, thicker skin. I leaned against the worn velvet cushions and reached for his hand. We said nothing for a long time. The surviving lamp lit only one corner of the big room, and in its feeble beacon, the heap of books looked like a natural feature; the chairs, feet up, like dead animals left long enough to swell. "I nearly shot Max once," I said. "At the cottage. This was in the fall after we'd moved back into town. I'd gone out with the kids to pick up something. I don't remember what, but I think a book. I saw Max's car in the drive, and I should have known, but I didn't. When I walked in, there he was with Beverly. The next thing I knew I had the .22 in my hand, the clip out of the drawer, and I was screaming that I was going to kill them both."

"Not the best move."

"Not my most rational moment. The thing is, I could have shot them. It could have been me. And Julie and Doug were there." I took a deep breath. "So I suppose I've felt I owed it to Max. He never mentioned what happened; he didn't use it during our divorce. Then there're the children. I wanted them to know it wasn't me."

"You don't really think they'd have—"

"You'd be surprised what you think about when people are murdered. The world tilts a hundred and eighty degrees and changes the way you look at everything."

There was a long silence.

"So now you know what Max knew. That I'm not easygoing, jolly Alice." I pressed his hand and released it. "Max was rather frightened, I think. Except in scholarship, he preferred superficiality. I suppose it would be fitting if that's what killed him, because that's where his heart was. I'd just always assumed it would be jealousy or rage."

"You assumed he'd be killed?" Sam asked, surprised.

"Not killed. Caught. I assumed he couldn't escape forever. I always saw that his life was on a collision course."

"So you left him."

"I left him because of what happened that day at the cottage. I didn't want to be that kind of person. I'd been crazy about Max—that was bad enough. I didn't want to be crazy any other way." I ran my hand through my hair. "The funny thing is, he didn't want a divorce. He'd been quite happy. You never know, do you?"

"No," he agreed, "Laura surprised me."

"I still think that someone surprised Max. And it's odd, I've had moments when I thought I knew. You know how you can't say a name but you know it's there somewhere in the chemistry, in the circuits. I keep thinking there's something I've overlooked, something I both know and don't know."

"Did he need money by any chance? Was he just a scholar or was he up to something else?"

"Like blackmail?"

"I'm just asking."

"I think not. That was where he didn't fool around, where he didn't compromise. He had his good points like the rest of us." I closed my eyes, the light replaced by blobs of remembered color.

"You should go to bed."

"Lot to do yet," I said. The books were still there, and

upstairs, clothes, papers, overturned furniture. Our business papers were scattered, everything in an uproar.

"Tomorrow," Sam said. He put his arm around my shoulder. "I'll stay if you like. Just in case."

"But just for just in case. I'm not up for anything else."

"That's obvious," he said. "Come on." I let him lead me
upstairs. I put the drawers back in my bureau and sat down
on my bed. Sam found a couple of broken lightbulbs and put
the fragments in the basket. "All right?" he asked.

I nodded, too exhausted to speak, and lay down on top of
the covers. The light went out. I heard him in the bathroom,
in the hall, then he settled on Doug's room. The last thing
I remembered was the sound of his shoes hitting the floor.

I woke up once, clawing up to consciousness with some dark
dream behind me, my heart pounding, my body slick with
sweat. The house was quiet with a difference, and it was a
struggle to remember that the children were gone, that Sam
was in Doug's bed. I walked down the moonlit hall to the
bathroom, where I splashed water on my face and changed
into my pajamas. Back in bed, I was embraced by dread: the
children were in danger, we'd lose the house and the business, I'd have to start again. I lay with my heart pounding
for a few minutes before exhaustion got the better of anxiety.
On the verge of sleep, I thought I had the answer, but it
slipped away, leaving only the awareness that there was no
way out except discovery. I'd have to find out what Max had
known and what he had planned to do with his knowledge.

At five the sky was gray with just the promise of light. I
pulled on a pair of jeans over my pajamas and went downstairs to straighten up the books. By the time the sun was
up, the living room was in order and I'd begun in our office,
sorting through folders, refiling bills and expense tallies, re-
arranging our small library of seed catalogs and herb suppli-
ers, of garden manuals and plant dictionaries. Around
six-thirty, I went down to feed Skipper and the cat and put
on the coffee. I stood under the shower for a few minutes,
then went into the kitchen and drank some juice. A golden

mist hung over the meadow, enlarging the trees with foggy halos. A thrush ascended the scale, and I thought, I'll do it. I'll manage. I'll have to. If I owed Max for the cottage, he owed me something too: and this was what I wanted.

Sam was coming out of the upstairs lav when I reached the landing with a second glass of juice. "I'm afraid I woke you," I said.

"Time," he said. "Today's the day to hook up the Becks' new fixtures, to start the Collins' piping, to look in on the leak in the Rodriguezes' washer. That for me?"

"Have it if you want," I said and handed over the glass.

"You look better. Up with the dawn."

"Dawn's my best time. What do you want for breakfast? You can have pancakes, bacon, eggs, fruit, cereal—whatever."

He set the glass down on the rail of the banister. "Pancakes with strawberries. No syrup."

"Easiest thing in the world if you feel like picking the berries."

He reached out and touched the side of my face lightly. "I'll get them in a minute," he said. "Do we have a minute?"

"What time do you have to be at the Becks'?"

"I promised first thing. But you know how those promises are."

"A little flexible?"

"A little flexible." He leaned over and kissed me, his touch gentle and eager. The window was too high to see the ruins of our farm; it showed only the golden morning, the sky starting to blue. I smiled and put my arms around him. "Give me a minute," I said.

▽

Chapter 12

SAM LEFT AROUND NINE-THIRTY, just before the vet reported that Dickins had survived the night and was running around on three legs and a lot of plaster. Detective Crombie reported that Warren Landis had decamped and that warrants were out for his arrest. I talked to the kids, who seemed to be finding life chez Todd an adventure, and I had only just gotten out to work with the remnants of the tomatoes, when the phone rang again. It was Herb.

"Alice! Alice, are you all right?" He was shouting.

"I'm all right, Herb. And I haven't gone deaf."

"You didn't call," he said.

"Things were chaotic here till late. State troopers all over the place. Moira's goats were killed. That was awful."

"Julie? Julie and Doug, where are they?"

"Safe," I said. "Neither was home at the time. Thank God."

"I mean now," he said, his voice rising. I realized Herb was frightened.

"Shaken up but okay," I said. "Listen, Herb, I'm on my way into Hartford to see the insurance people. I'll look in, okay?"

"Alice, I'm due in court at one. Can you make it before then?"

119

I said I could but it was after twelve before I got to his office. Although there was only time for a courtesy call, I was shown in immediately. Herb came around his desk and kissed me on the cheek. "Jesus, Alice! We've got to get things under control. Are you really all right?"

"Yes. Although my life's a bit of a muddle at the moment." I thought of the latest complication, of a particular half hour earlier in the morning, and suppressed a smile.

"I must say you are taking this calmly. All I could think about were the kids. Where are they, for God's sake?"

"Out of harm's way."

"Alice! The children? After all, I'm their trustee."

"Moira took them. They'll be all right."

"I thought Moira was still with you."

"She has friends. If the police don't get things sorted out in a day or two, I may have to send them to Max's parents. We'll see."

Herb walked back around his desk. "Fine kids," he said. His hand strayed toward his row of pictures, and then I saw what I should have seen a week ago. I caught my breath and sat down abruptly. Herb turned and gave me a quick look.

"Aftereffects," I said. He thought out loud for a few minutes, speculating on what the insurance would do for us and about whether or not we would be repaid for bringing a civil suit against "the perpetrators."

"Assuming they're caught," I said.

"We've got to be optimistic," he said.

Right. Optimistic, not panicked. It couldn't have been Herb, not Herb with his love of children. Couldn't have been.

His secretary opened the door, and he asked, "What is it, Phyllis?"

Her voice was low, a professional murmur.

"Excuse me, Alice," he said. Whatever the call was, he'd decided to take it in the outer office. I heard the door close. Heard another door open and close, heard the unintelligible rumble of Herb's voice. I was standing alone by the desk, and I didn't think twice. I reached out and plucked a snap of a pretty girl with curly black hair from the corner of one frame. I was closing my purse as Herb opened the door.

"I've got to go to court," he said. He sounded tired. I had not noticed before that Herb has sad eyes. "Think over your options, Alice. You can call me anytime."

"All right."

"And the children," he added. "Remember me to the children."

I took the long way home and stopped to see Eunice at the post office. I bought a sheet of commemoratives and drew out the photo with the money.

"Your girl!" Eunice exclaimed. "My, she's pretty."

"I was forgetting—you'd mentioned she'd been in with Max?"

"Yes, just before—poor Mr. Bertram. He was so proud of her. Lovely girl."

"Yes," I said, but I could feel myself losing contact with previous assumptions.

"Are you all right, Mrs. Bertram?"

"It's been a long day," I said picking up my stamps. "Thanks."

"Your picture," she said.

"Forget my head . . ." I joked, but I wasn't thinking about evidence or pictures or even about Max romancing his best friend's teenager. I was thinking that I'd as much as told Herb Rosen where the children were. Of course, he probably hadn't shot Max, Bev, and Timmy. I was rational enough to know that. But he'd had a motive, and in my present state of mind, that was enough. I called Moira from the phone booth in the village, got Todd instead, and explained the problem. "I think I should come down and get the kids," I said.

"And take them where?"

"That's the trouble. Max's parents would love to have them, but my mother-in-law isn't very well."

"Where do they live?"

"Out in Pittsburgh."

"You'd have to get a flight. There's probably not more than

one a day. It's what—three-thirty or so? You might not get one today as it is."

"Yes, I know."

"How do you feel about the child labor laws?"

"Excuse me?"

"Child labor. Best place to hide them. Moira's perhaps mentioned my new restaurant down the coast?"

She had indeed! "I think she told me something."

"Nouvelle cuisine but still tasty, American food. Recognizable, you know."

"I'm always in favor of recognizable food."

"Fresh, healthy, but not 'health food.' That's what I'm aiming for at Steak and Sprouts. Doing real well too."

"Doug and Julie," I said.

"Where do they fit in? Moira didn't approve when I first suggested this, but I think now you'll see the beauty of it. Steak and Sprouts, being new to the area, has been short of staff."

"You need busboys," I said.

"Right. And waitresses, kitchen help. Two sweet, good-looking kids. Hey, can I use them?"

"What sort of hours?" I asked. "No, forget that. It's a good idea. But where would they sleep?"

"My sister's been running the place out of a little apartment, living over the store, so to speak. For a few days, I think, okay. More than that—"

"I hope it won't be more than a couple of days in any case. The police tell me they have some leads. Some of the neighbors saw the truck. If it's longer, we'll make other arrangements."

"That's fine."

"I really appreciate this, Todd. I know it's an imposition."

"Listen, what Moira wants, Moira gets. And I'm short of help. That's for real."

"That's super. Maybe I'd better talk to Julie and Doug. Just to get things straightened out." I anticipated problems, protests, discontent, but when they came on the line, they were both excited. Doug was caught up in the idea of going undercover and seemed completely consoled for his banishment from school, while Julie was taken with the compensation, which was a big step up from her pittance at the stable. "You be careful," I said. "Stay out of sight. And don't give Todd's sister any trouble." "Mind your manners and take care" was inadequate, but what else to say? They promised the earth and hung up. I drove home, put on my work clothes, and went out to the garden.

In some ways it looked worse partially cleaned up. Big bare patches like horticultural mange splotched the beds, and some of the plants marked as survivors were beginning to go limp and soft, damaged in the roots, maybe, or shocked by sudden violence. Moira had decided on a new strawberry patch and had begun setting out rootlets salvaged from the main bed. I continued the work, discarding mangled plants, dividing the good ones, and planting young offshoots. This done, I spread the bed with clean hay for mulch and moved on to the next section. By five-thirty, I'd finished a big rectangle. The pale gray-gold hay made a pleasing contrast with the brown earth and dark green plants. Amidst the wreckage, the new plot looked reassuringly neat and shipshape. Things could be set to rights. Life was basically orderly, and hard work would enable us to suppress inconvenient information—such as the fact that Herb Rosen had a motive and might have had knowledge of what Max was doing.

Satisfied with the progress of the garden, I took Skipper down the road for a walk, then had a shower. I was drying my hair when the phone rang, and I put down the towel and listened to the sound in the empty house. My first impulse was to let it ring, to let the answering machine record. Then I thought about the kids, Moira and Sam and went into the kitchen and lifted the receiver.

"Mrs. Bertram?"

"Hello?"

"You're being foolish," the voice said. It was not Warren Landis. It was a low voice, professionally bland, without accent or region, like a television announcer's.

"Who is this?" My voice, on the other hand, was strained, pitched high, frightened. I should have hung up.

"A concerned friend. You ought to mind your own business, Mrs. Bertram. If you want your children to be safe."

I'd been aware of crazy spells lately, times when I lost perspective or control—or both—and this was one of them. "Just a minute, you goddamned bastard," I shouted into the receiver. "If you've got anything to say to me, you come in person." I went on in this vein, swearing and crying, until I realized that the line had gone dead. I leaned my forehead against the wall and listened to my galloping heart. It was a few minutes before I could call the police, who said that they would see what could be done through the phone company, and Sam, whose answering machine promised to return my call. The house was suddenly intolerable, and I drove back up to the village, called the children from the public phone, got Moira instead, and learned that they were already on their way to Steak and Sprouts. "Everything's fine here," Moira said, and, unreasonably, that irritated me, too. Irritated me enough so that I took the long way home past Sam's house, saw his truck, and wound up sharing steak and french fries and cauliflower in cheese sauce.

"Now, if we only had some of your apple pie," Sam said.

"If things ever get back to normal, that's the first order of business."

"Soon," he said. "Surely things will be taken seriously now."

"Seriously. But not connected—not to what happened to Max, with Max."

"Too much invested in the original theory?"

"Not even that. It's a case of not even seeing anything else. And, of course, that's how they look at me—as someone who only sees one side, one picture."

"And not enough evidence, maybe?"

"Not a plausible scenario." I pushed the cutlery around on the table. "The other day—when I found the goats and everything—I had the thought that that's what had happened to Max. I mean, that he'd come home to find blood and everything ruined."

"But he was apparently shot with the same caliber weapon."

"I don't mean that he killed himself—though I thought of that. I mean that he might have come home while whoever did it was ransacking the house—and holding Bev and Timmy in the main bedroom. Remember that they were both shot on the master bed. That seemed odd to me. As if they'd been cowering there."

"Afraid of Max, in the official theory."

"Or of someone unknown, in my version, yes. Now Max kept the .22 by the back door. The clip was in the chest in the living room. We'd had a lot of rats originally and, later, when we put in a garden, rabbits and woodchucks. Not that he ever hit very many—and after the kids were bigger he didn't dare kill anything—but he'd bang away and frighten them off."

"Did that weapon ever show up?"

"No. First, the police said it was in with the evidence, then they said it wasn't. Now they say that it never was there, that he must have traded it in when he went on that non-existent gun-shopping trip."

Sam shrugged. "It's not impossible that he got rid of it."

"No. But my thought is that he arrived at the wrong moment. That he walked in, picked up the .22, and precipitated the killings. Otherwise, it doesn't make sense. It's too elaborate and too much and the destruction the other day isn't enough, if you see what I mean."

"No big, careful plot. Just incompetence?"

"Or panic. Bad timing. Bad judgment."

"It's the way most things get done. But they have the gun dealer's word."

"And his records. But they're not Holy Writ."

Sam nodded. "Aside from that, it makes sense. Assuming their MO was the same. You were lucky, Alice. You and Moira and the children."

"Don't I know it."

"Me, too. Very lucky."

I smiled at him and thought, this is a good moment. "I stopped by tonight with an ulterior motive."

"I hope so."

"Well, that too, but I'd like to have another look at the cottage. You know more about guns than I do."

"You want to go looking for .22 slugs?"

"Yes. Fired from somewhere in the front hall or the doorway to the living room."

"Be a bit dark."

"The power's still on. The police were there and looking about, then the cleaners, and the realtor's been in and out with people. We just left the electricity on."

"All right. Why don't you take your car home? I'll meet you at your house and drive you over."

The cottage was about a half hour away, and it was nearly dark before we pulled into the lane. "Quiet area," Sam said. I'd forgotten that he'd never been there.

"The state forest starts half a mile in that direction. The rest is farmland. The cottage has twelve acres, more or less, between the road and the stream."

"Good land?"

"I think so. We always had a good garden."

Sam parked the car on the drive and stepped out. "So this belongs to you?"

"Yes, Max bought it for me, really. It was in my name. I didn't want it after the divorce, and I was quite willing to sign it over to him, but Max never did anything about it. The problem will be selling it."

"Or keeping it?"

"Not the house. I couldn't live in the house. Not now." I took the key out of my pocket and unlocked the front door. The cottage smelled musty, vaguely damp, and I walked around opening windows and turning on the lights.

"Where—uh—did it happen?" Sam asked. The cleaners had been in to remove the chalk circles that had ghosted the dead, the stains on the floors, and the blood-soaked rugs.

"Max died here." I traced a line on the living-room floor. "Bev and Timmy were killed in the main bedroom through there. I had them remove the bed. Everything else will have to be sold. The bureau and such."

"The police say he shot them, then went into the living room and killed himself?"

"That's right. And they found bullets in the bodies that matched the gun. But they didn't find any extras. I tried to tell them that Max was an awful shot. Truly awful. They seemed to feel he might have improved."

"Where did he keep the .22?" Sam asked.

"Here. Right here in the hallway. He carried on a vendetta with the rats in the shed. Clip was here, gun by the door, shoot from the porch." I shook my head. "Never hit any."

"I'll come in the door," Sam said. "Pick up the gun—which drawer for the clip?"

"Top left."

"Let's check," he said. "See how long it would have taken."

"Right. And I'll go into the bedroom, where I'm watching Bev and the boy. There should have been two. One to watch, one to search."

"Let's see if this is right, first. They'd have heard the car—when?"

"Maybe not at all. It's muddy here in the spring. Max sometimes parked out by the road."

"Was that where they found his car?"

"No. But it would have made sense to bring it back out of sight later."

"That might have given him time. Otherwise—"

"We'll see," I said. I went into the bedroom, listened for Sam to return to the porch. The seconds flashed on my watch. One, two . . . at three I was in the living room, and Sam was coming through the front door.

"I think only if he walked in."

"Maybe not then. I'm here, if I'm armed . . ."

"Would they necessarily have seen the rifle?"

"That's another thing. It was against the wall, behind that chest."

"So, he comes in," Sam said. "What then?"

"Indignation and bravado," I said without a moment's hesitation. "Max loved a scene."

"He was brave?"

I hesitated. "I don't know. Do we ever know, outside of the situation? But there was a bit of playacting in Max. He loved drama. He'd have loved the risk, even the being-afraid of it."

"And would he have recognized the real thing?"

"Soon. He was sharp."

"He comes in," Sam said, "either grabs the gun immediately or when he gets a chance. Then he has to get the clip from the drawer."

"Unless he'd started carrying it."

"He'd have been here," said Sam. "Stand in the doorway. That's the only other entrance to the room—so."

"This wall and this one. Max wasn't reliable with the gun."

We started going along the walls, squinting against the light, touching the plaster, searching for bullets. Sam went out and got a flashlight in the hope of picking up any flaw in the wall, and I found the stepstool and looked up near the molding. I'd covered most of the back wall, when I saw a tiny round black mark on the ceiling.

"Sam."

"Any luck?"

"Have a look at this," I said, and let him have the stepstool.

"Bingo!" he glanced over his shoulder. "Hell of an angle." He took out a little knife and probed gently. "Do we take it out? It could be one of the other slugs."

"I think mark where it was and take it out. There may be more."

"We'll hope so. There being no official witnesses."

"I'm sick of officials," I said. "Let me hold the light."

He probed away, dropping little flecks of plaster and paint. "Going to make a mess of this wallboard."

"Never mind that."

"Ah." He held a bullet up to the light and nodded. I held out my hand, and he dropped a small two-toned slug, flattened at the tip, onto my palm. "Good guess," he said.

We found two more, circled them, and left them embedded, one more in the ceiling, one in the wall. Sam stood in the living room, staring at the marks and moving back and forth. "I'd say here," he said finally. "I'd say he fired from here. And if they turn up the rifle, they can prove it fired the shots."

He was five or six feet from the bureau, a couple of feet from where Max was found. It was possible.

"He came home and found them," I said.

Sam nodded, and I knelt on the floor and touched the boards. It had not been real to me before. Or real, but not credible, not vivid. I could smell the goats' blood, and in their cries and their frenzy, I started to cry for Max. Sam put his hand on my shoulder and didn't say anything.

"Sorry," I said after a few minutes and wiped my face on my sleeve.

"Have a paper towel," Sam said, handing me a wad torn from the roll in the kitchen.

"Thanks."

"You'll call the police?" he asked. Sam's getting to know me.

"Tomorrow. That's enough for today."

"Let's go," he said.

On the way home, he asked if I wanted a drink.

"What are you offering?"

"Scotch, beer. I think there's a little bourbon."

"Scotch," I said. "Scotch and sympathy is what I need. In fact you can hold the scotch."

"Sympathy's my long suit," Sam said easily, but back in his house there was an awkwardness between us, the shadow of grief or of Max, and I was home before ten. I brought Skipper into the house, put the clip in Sam's gun, and took both it and the dog upstairs.

Chapter 13

MOIRA AND I SPENT the next morning hard at work, resulting in a pretty thorough cleanup and a dozen flats of salvaged plants to sell.

"We're going to go broke," I said by way of conversation.

"You've talked to the insurance?"

"Oh, sure. And there'll be something. Sometime." The law's delay is nothing compared to an insurance giant with its heels dug in. "What I need to know is, are we selling these or declaring immediate bankruptcy?"

"We have to pay Dickins's bills," Moira said. "Better sell."

"Right."

"The vet said he might be able to come home next week." She leaned against her shovel and studied the edge of the meadow. "I've been checking around with goat breeders. To see about selling Dickins. Once he's well, that is."

"So this is it?"

"Oh, shit, Alice, I don't know. Financially, it's going to be awful tough. And frankly, thinking of the long term, it's a bit of a commute. That house is a white elephant, and we have more barn than we need. I know you love it, but it was always too big a place for the two of us. I just don't know."

"We might be able to sell it to some small farmer. I'd hate

to see it subdivided. I keep thinking maybe the cottage will sell. Or something else will come through."

"You're dreaming, Alice."

"I've been told that before," I said, gathering up my hoe and shovel.

"Where are you going?"

"To sell the flats. You'd better start making an inventory. If we're to be out of here, we'll have to sell the whole thing."

"Alice," she said, but I didn't look back. I had the flats in the truck and the truck on the road damn quick. When I got back around eleven-thirty, I found the phone ringing. It was Doreen, and she didn't sound happy. "I want to talk to you."

"All right. Do you want me to stop by your dorm this afternoon?"

"No," she said quickly. "There's a health food restaurant near campus."

When I said I knew the one, she said, "Noon," and hung up. I was there promptly. Having tried and failed a second time to contact Crombie, I took the truck back out and pulled into the restaurant right at twelve. In better times, I'd have marked it down as a potential customer and introduced myself to the owner. In present troubles, I contented myself with studying the menu. Doreen arrived as I was ordering a cup of soup. "One for you?" I asked.

"Yeah, sure, the asparagus," she said, though she didn't look hungry. What she looked was nervous. I couldn't decide if that was a good sign or not.

We sat down next to the cascade of greenery that all but blocked the front window. Although she'd been in a major hurry when she'd called, Doreen showed no inclination to open the conversation, and halfway through my tomato and lentil, I said, "Why did you want to see me?"

"I saw the story in the paper."

"Yeah. Nasty business. They're looking for Warren Landis—he was Bev's husband."

"Yes," said Doreen. She shook her golden mane and folded her arms protectively across her chest. "I was down by the river this morning. Damn Friedland wanted some new sam-

ples. When I got there, I found troopers' cars all over the
place. The river road was blocked with an ambulance, police
photographer—everything. They found a body up in back—
near where Max and I saw the hiker." She stopped and ran
a nervous hand across her face.

That suggested all kinds of things, none of them nice.
"Any idea who?"

She shook her head. "Nobody was saying anything. I wish
I'd never met your damn husband." Max certainly hadn't
brought any of us luck.

"You said you and Max saw the hiker. You didn't tell me
that."

"I didn't tell you everything," she said.

"How can you be sure it was the same man?"

"It was him all right. The right day, everything. We were
up above the river when we passed this guy, tough looking,
with two others."

"So he wasn't alone?"

"He wasn't a hiker, either. Max acted as if he recognized
one of them, though he didn't say anything. Later, when the
fellow was reported missing, he said it was important not
to let on we knew. That it would hurt what he was working
on. He said that he was close to having everything he
needed."

"Which had something to do with the river?"

"Yes."

"And explained his sudden interest in hiking."

"That was a combination of things," Doreen said a trifle
smugly. "But yes, he was interested in the dumping angle. I
figured that out later. I remember that he asked me about
United Biologicals—I gather there is some question about
them now."

"He didn't go into any more detail?"

"You knew Max," she said.

"Yes," I said.

"There's something else," she said. "I wasn't going to
bother. I mean, what was it to me? But the robbery, then
your house being trashed—that was too much. Anyway,

there's a manuscript—I suppose that's been the motive for the robbery and everything."

"You mean something other than the book on the Salisburys? I have what he finished of that."

"I don't know what it was about. Max talked in generalities. He said he was writing a 'great American tragedy.' He was very excited about it, but closemouthed."

"A book about the river?"

"No, no. That was just peripheral. No, it was something in his own field."

"But you don't know where it is?"

"He'd gotten very paranoid, very worried. He kept saying that he could influence the next election, that this book showed all the weaknesses of the process."

"You say he seemed paranoid. What do you mean by that?"

"Just what the word means," she said irritably. "He thought that he was in danger, that there were people who wanted to destroy his work and him too."

"And did you believe him?"

She shrugged. "Not entirely. Max was always so dramatic, so theatrical. But he did seem nervous."

"Did he talk about protecting himself? About buying a weapon, for example?"

"No. Though he did buy one, didn't he?"

I decided not to mention my theory about the rifle. "Anything else?"

"He said the manuscript was safe. You know how he was always sending off packages of videotape?"

"He exchanged political speeches and rallies and so on with other poli-sci people."

"Around the world. Must have been a horrendous bill for postage," Doreen said. "Anyway, one day he said, 'It's safe for a while. I've been to the post office.' He was talking about the manuscript."

"Do you think he sent it to a publisher, perhaps?"

"No, I don't think so. It wasn't finished. He said it was 'off for safekeeping.' I wasn't paying too much attention, but I thought he meant he'd sent it overseas somewhere."

"To one of his video people?"

"I think so."

"None of this was ever brought out. It might have made an enormous difference to the investigation. For one thing it provides someone other than Max with a motive."

Doreen made a little gesture with her hands. Like the rest of her, they looked strong and capable. "I wasn't in love with Max," she said. "I never had any illusions about him. He was nice in bed but totally self-centered. He wanted something from me—information, my research notes. He convinced himself he was crazy about me to make sure of getting them. I didn't care—he was never boring—but I wasn't going to take risks for him. And I'm not now. I'm leaving this afternoon. I told Friedland I wasn't well and needed a break. I'll come back when all this quiets down."

"Fair enough. But what were the risks for Max?"

"I don't know, but he was frightened. Make that, he was frightened and excited by it. By danger, by the thought of doing dangerous things, important things. He got so caught up in it that I didn't take him too seriously, because I could see how much he liked drama. Then—you know—everything else happened and I panicked."

"Had he actually been afraid of losing his life?"

"So he said. One day he said that there was someone he could have trusted with the manuscript, if he hadn't had to think of the kids. His idea was to send it off until he had the whole thing done. Once it got out, got published, he said he'd be all right. If anything happened to him then, it would be too obvious. He said they'd never risk it once the book was in print. That's what he thought," she said, getting up from the table abruptly. "Listen, that's all I can tell you."

"One other thing," I said. "Warren Landis. Did Max ever talk about him?"

"Max never mentioned shit," she said. "He asked the questions, he didn't give any answers. Take my advice—forget him and protect yourself. That's what I'm going to do."

I thanked her for the good counsel, but as soon as I got home, I went to the barn for the boxes with Max's office stuff and took out his Rolodex. His calendar had been missing and his notes, and there were apparently reasons for their absence. But the Rolodex had been left as harmless. I started with the As, writing down names and cross-checking against our old address book. A post-doc on exchange from Japan seemed likely—I remembered Dr. Choki as a pretty woman well-versed in the art of concealing determination under compliance. Then there was an Italian, Professor Bennetti, a specialist in Fascism who told funny stories about the private lives of politicians. He'd come for a family picnic one day. Max had kept in touch, too, with an Oxford don, a dry, rather timid type whose prose was angelic, and with a young Australian who'd camped with us for a few weeks when his living arrangements went awry. Pritchert had come with a crying baby and a harried young wife, and for weeks afterward our house had smelled of diapers and heated milk.

The Australian only brought me to the Ps. Generous and gregarious, Max had brought home strays and lions indiscriminately. I was beginning to get disheartened at the number of his potential video friends, but the idea of the manuscript was irresistible, and by four-thirty I had winnowed the list down to twenty names I considered possible.

With this in hand, I phoned Eunice at our former post office, explaining that Max had mailed out a manuscript a few weeks before his death. "I just learned of its existence, and we can't find another copy. I hate to bother you, but it's probably valuable."

"I'm sure," she said. Eunice takes a proprietary interest in her customers, and the idea that any manuscript of Professor Bertram's might not be valuable would have struck her as deeply offensive.

"I've been going through his Rolodex—nine hundred and eighty names, Eunice! I don't want to start writing everyone—"

"End the postal deficit."

"I'm afraid my patriotism doesn't go that far. I wondered if you'd recognize any of these?" I read off my list of names and addresses.

"Hmmm," she said. "He sent to Japan regularly. Video-tapes, airmail."

"Just videotape?"

"Yes, all small packages, and the German one too. Two or three tapes at a time."

"Anything manuscript-size?"

"Yes. Not long ago. But not to either of them. What was that Australian address?"

I repeated it.

"It went to the Australian. I think I mentioned that the professor had come in with your daughter and some packages."

"And they were his packages?"

"Oh, yes. He had a little sticker with his name on it."

"I see. Thank you very much, Eunice."

I hung up the phone as the adrenaline kicked in. So much that had seemed fanciful, unrealistic, frankly crazy had turned out to be true: there was a manuscript. A manuscript that contained something worth breaking up our house for, maybe something worth killing Max for. I was itching to call Pritchert, but when I checked the time difference to Perth, I realized I could hardly call him before dawn. I waited impatiently until supper was over. We seemed to be getting an unusually nice spring, and it was a lovely, mild evening. I sat by the upstairs phone, looking out at the pale apple trees, each with a circle of fallen blossoms whitening the grass beneath. A skein of geese went over, honking resonantly, and in the woodlot a thrush began to sing. There was a gurgle on the line, the sound of switches closing, then a phone rang, ridiculously clear and close. A woman answered. I asked to speak to David Pritchert and a moment later, I recognized the voice, the nasal vowels overlaid with British university. But he no longer sounded young and harried. Max's Rolodex had said "Professor," and he sounded relaxed and self-assured.

"David, it's Alice Bertram."

"Good Lord! I should have known when Mabel said 'from the States.' How are you?"

"Only so-so," I said. Then I asked if he'd heard about

Max. He hadn't, and I had to recount the whole dismal story.

"I didn't know," he kept saying. "It'll be in the journals later, of course. Alice, this is so extraordinary, I'd have called before had I known. I just didn't take it too seriously."

"What, David?"

"Of course, you don't know! He sent me a parcel—when—six weeks ago, maybe? A new manuscript. He asked me to keep it for a while until he asked for it. In case something happened to him."

"That's what he said?"

"Yes. In case anything happened to him, I was to send it on to you at—something farm, is that right?"

"Yes. Old Fields Farm. That's where I'm living now."

"I didn't know what he was talking about, but of course I've kept it safe."

"What's the book about?"

"It's entitled *The Decline and Fall of an American Political Family*. A first draft, a bit rough in spots, as you'd guess, but, Alice, quite brilliant, quite, quite brilliant."

"You've read it then?"

"With great interest. It's a classic story—the old political family whose economic base can no longer support their political ambitions. They can't stand their decline and sell their souls to recoup their lost influence."

"Sounds as if they marry money."

His laugh bounced off some distant satellite and rattled in my ear. "Out of style! According to Max they—or at least the youngest of them—attached themselves to a couple of shady characters. But gradually, that's the genius of it. A few thousand here, a daughter's wedding party there, then a little stock in a mob company, then a little more, until finally the heir apparent moves to Florida, becomes a developer, and a U.S. senator."

John Salisbury III! Max's patron. Commissioner of the family history. "And the implication is that he was staked by mob money?"

"Very clearly. The last section is sketchy and there's possibly some more on the computer disks and note cards. I didn't want to go through—well, personal papers, but I thought the manuscript was all right. I mean, since he'd sent it to me, I assumed he'd wanted me to read it."

"David, you've got the only complete copy. Could you fax me that last section on John Salisbury III, the Florida senator? I can't tell you how important it might be. And also would you duplicate the manuscript from the Depression Era on and send me that section of the original by express mail? I'll pay you back."

"My pleasure, but don't worry about the bill. Listen, I haven't forgotten the summer we stayed with you. It'll be done first thing today."

"Thanks. I really appreciate that."

"Alice."

"Yes?"

"He was afraid for his life. I thought he was just being funny or being dramatic, but it's clear that he meant what he said."

"Yes," I said. "I believe that. In a sense I've been counting on that."

There was a pause. "I see," he said. "Well, in that case, be careful, Alice."

I thanked him, hung up, and waited impatiently until, just minutes before closing time, the little general store up in the village called to say that I had received a long fax message from Australia. That night, I got into bed with the missing chapters of Max's tame, authorized family portrait of the Salisburys, and found out that my former husband had not been so easily bought.

What David Pritchert had sent me began with an account of the long, slow Salisbury retrenchment. In the recession of the seventies, the lavish Victorian mansion (now being, I recalled, reopened and refurbished) was abandoned, the last of their mills was closed, and the assets sold off to another corporation. Despite producing a distinguished state senator, the family was withdrawing from productive and political life. There were no more Salisbury entrepreneurs. They tended their stocks, enjoyed society, did good works.

Then came John III, who moved to Florida, became a developer, and met interesting friends, friends without two hundred and fifty plus years of living well and doing good, friends not lucky enough to have had an ancestor who shorted the Union troops. One of those friends was Robert Tomcarelli, trucking heir, art patron extraordinaire, and a social climber both ruthless and ingenious; another was Martin Forgette, who was interested in politics and whose wife, Caroline, was not only principal stockholder in United Biologicals but also a distant cousin of Suzi Tomcarelli's.

I had to admit that these were interesting friendships for a scion of the elegant and reserved Salisburys. The Forgettes and Tomcarellis lived high in all the right places and enjoyed themselves without worrying overmuch about vulgarity. Max had tracked them through the glossy magazines that specialize in the rich at play and followed their fortunes in the *Wall Street Journal*. So far as he was able, that is. Like the Salisburys, the Tomcarellis and Forgettes were inbred and interconnected: friends, family, and business formed a series of interlocking relationships where not everything had to be committed to paper or overseen by lawyers. Max had left several handwritten notations "to check this" or "ask Wolfe," whom I took to be the reporter Chester Wolfe, who had tried unsuccessfully to contact me after the robbery.

Added to the rest of the manuscript, Max's concluding chapters had an almost novelistic appeal; after earnest, uncomplicated struggles for survival, after status and achievement and enormous wealth came decline and a corrupt resurrection via tainted wealth. But that fiscal miracle was both subtle and ambiguous. John III met the Tomcarellis first—on the opera board I'd guess, though Max mentioned tennis lessons, to which both Suzi Tomcarelli and John's wife, Vivian, were addicted. When the Salisburys moved to Florida, they found the Tomcarellis their winter neighbors in Palm Beach. When the Salisbury daughter was eighteen, the Tomcarellis loaned their splendid house for a coming-out party—and probably footed the bills. And when the Salisbury development company hit hard times with high infla-

tion rates in the late seventies, the Tomcarellis stepped in,
bought an interest (perhaps with the Forgettes' cash) and
tided the firm over. They had been good friends to John and
Vivian.

Perhaps genuinely—there was a touch of Gatsby as well
as Godfather about the Tomcarellis, at least in Max's account. I saw that my late ex had had an aesthetic under-
standing of personality, that he saw complexity, that he was
capable of empathy—on paper, at least. In person, with the
exception of children, whom he always treated kindly, Max
had seemed indifferent to others except when they served
his ends. He'd been charming but exploitive, sensitive but
manipulative, so it was with a certain surprise that I read
his delicate explanation of the relations between the Salisburys and these other families, who were, in a sense, Salisburys of an earlier period—the buccaneers of Civil War
profiteering or the tough and perhaps savage pioneers. Even
if there were details missing, informants to be tracked down,
i's to be dotted and t's crossed, the outline was still clear.
Out of a mix of personal attraction and social ambitions, the
Tomcarellis of unsavory business and mob connections had
seduced the Salisburys, whose ten generations of prosperity
and influence had left them with the desperate pride of declining aristocrats. And once the Salisburys were caught, or
from the other point of view, once the Salisburys were back
on their feet financially, the Forgettes—of larger view, deeper
purse, and more dangerous ambition than their cousins—
recognized the politician's utility.

Max had that. I found that he knew all about the contracts
secured, the favors done. In ten years, United Biologicals had
gone from a purveyor of formaldehyde-soaked tapeworms,
crayfish, and frogs to a giant of the specialized-waste-han-
dling industry. A good deal of highly paid work had been
funneled to UB by its beneficiary, now its benefactor, Senator
Salisbury and by his Connecticut-based brother, Toby. There
were contracts that had evaded public bidding and rumors
of campaign contributions that had eluded detection. And
still to come, but "in the pipeline": superfund contracts,

weapons plant cleanups, detoxification of buildings, streams, dumps, ground—a mesh of profit, influence, and expertise. UB and the Forgettes were making the most of their contacts—to make money and, Max hinted, to avoid paying out more than they needed—and the Tomcarellis, who'd snared this golden goose, went along for the ride. All this Max knew.

There was only one thing he did not know, though he had suspected and had endeavored, via the gorgeous and clear-headed Doreen Hale, to turn up the goods. Though against all his tastes, he had tramped the woods and hiked by the river. Though he had—was it for this?—risked his life. But I knew, and I found an ironic rightness about the fact: I knew that the connections between United Biologicals and Tomco Trucking, between the Forgettes and the Tomcarellis, went beyond kinship and society into mutual profit. I knew that the Tomcarellis had not changed their stripes, that while the glitter of their lives could obscure the origin of their wealth, their business practices were not so easily altered. The trucks along the river and at Konkret Kast, the shots, and most important, the presence of one clean little UB van in the Tomco lot—that was what Max had needed. The relationship between Senator Salisbury and his backers was not only ill-advised, it was corrupt. Worse than most? Perhaps not, but the handsome senator who said innocuous things about the environment and preened himself on four generations of public service would have some explaining to do. Enough explaining, I thought, so that his chances of higher office might be pretty unlikely. Enough, so that big, new government contracts for UB could be jeopardized and the last rarified bastions of society closed to the Tomcarellis.

Yes, my husband had learned enough to be awkward. But enough to murder three people, including a child of seven? I wasn't so sure. I thought I'd like to talk to Chester Wolfe, whom Max apparently had trusted, and the next morning, after I put a note about the .22 slugs and a copy of the fax in the mail to Detective Crombie, I drove into Hartford.

▽

Chapter 14

THE NEWSPAPER'S OFFICES WERE large, modern, and elegant. There was a quarter acre or so of forced chrysanthemums, plus ivies and tropicals. There were blowups of schoolkids using the local rag in educational settings, and there was even a little glass shopfront at one side of the lobby that sold t-shirts and a variety of small souvenirs should one wish to commemorate one's visit. I decided I'd pass on that for the moment, gave my name, and asked if I could speak to Chester Wolfe. While the guard shifted her gum and phoned upstairs, I checked out the nearest plants for signs of white fly and mildew.

"He'll be right down. Fill out a badge."

As soon as I had written my name, destination, and license number, the reporter appeared. He was very tall and gangly, with a lot of untidy brown hair, round horn-rimmed glasses, and a drooping Zapata mustache that made him look less dashing than depressed. "Chester Wolfe," he said, extending a nicotine-stained hand. His voice was no more than a whisper over the clatter on the tile floors and the muted hubbub of the nearby offices, and when he bent his long body so that his face was close to mine, he looked like a fanatical anarchist.

"Alice Bertram. I think you knew my ex-husband. He was working on—"

"I knew Max," he interrupted. "I knew Max pretty well, and I liked him pretty much." His look was defiant.

"Is there somewhere we could talk?"

He looked vaguely around the lobby, then loped off toward the elevators, motioning for me to follow with one of his large, yellowed hands. On the second floor, he led me through a maze of cubicles and passages to a tiny office, white and spartan, undecorated except for a poster with a drawing of Trotsky. My heart sank. I'd guessed right: a conspirator, a paranoid. And then I thought, why not? Mr. Wolfe just might understand my point of view. There was a second chair half-hidden under piles of magazines and releases. I put these on the floor and sat down. "Max came to see you about the book he was writing."

"That's right. Max was a brilliant writer—and a fine person."

"Max was a brilliant writer and a son of a bitch. But he was neither homicidal nor suicidal."

The wary eyes behind the thick glasses met mine for the first time.

"As well to put our cards on the table," I said.

"All right." He reached across his desk for a narrow, spiral-bound reporter's notebook and began toying with a pencil.

"You cover politics? You didn't cover the—the criminal case."

"No. But I kept up with it. I'd known Max for a while. I was a student of his, actually."

"And he had come to you for help with his book. You knew he was writing a book?"

Chester Wolfe smiled for the first time. "I guessed Max was writing a book. He was closemouthed about the project."

"Yes, and that was atypical—a tip-off that something was odd. He'd nearly completed the manuscript before he died. He'd been keeping his computer disks—and probably the manuscript—hidden in an old well at the cottage. The cottage we used to own in—"

"I remember," Chester said quickly, and I thought better of him because he found this awkward, almost as awkward as I did.

"That last week he mailed off the manuscript, complete except for a few gaps and questions—some for you—to a friend in Australia. That's how I got hold of it. The Australian said that Max had been afraid for his life."

"Do you believe that?" Wolfe asked quickly.

My eyes wandered to the ink drawing of Trotsky—a virtuosic swirl of seemingly random lines that knotted and congealed into eyebrows, nose, the corner of a lip like the essence of mystery. "Max had a great imagination," I said. "He loved pretending, loved secrets and puzzles."

"He used to do one class a semester on historical mysteries."

"I'm trying to decide if he had reason for this one. He may have. He'd apparently considered leaving the manuscript with me, but was concerned about the children. Max's concern for me was never an item," I added and immediately regretted it. I sounded sour. The woman scorned.

"Was the book about Senator Salisbury?"

"About the whole family—back to Amos and Sarah in the eighteenth century. The tricky parts were about the Honorable from Florida."

"And about his friends?"

"Yes, particularly his friends."

"So," said Chester Wolfe, "what can I do?"

I took out the manuscript and showed him Max's questions.

"We'll have to check the morgue files. Max looked through them earlier when he was just starting." The greenish fluorescent light glinted off the reporter's glasses. "Tomcarelli and Forgette—we have files on them for sure. Salisbury, of course, but there'll be nothing Max didn't already have."

We'd gotten the folders and were sitting at one of the big Formica tables when I thought to ask for Herb Rosen's too.

"Good idea," Wolfe said, nodding his shaggy head. "It seems to me he was—well, we'll see. I'll fill out the form for it."

I thanked him and started through the folders. Most of the Tomcarelli and Forgette material was already familiar from the conclusion of Max's manuscript. It added up to a three-part melange of society, business, and chicanery. Here were notes about illegal dumping, toxic waste, and inadequate sewage treatment, plus rumors of extortion, complaints from customers, and nasty details of the urban haulage wars. There were violations and citations and fines. Protests, rebuttals, appeals. There was enough dirt about both Tomco and UB to give even the casual reader pause—if the casual reader ever did pause—instead of being swamped in charges and responses, in indignant denials and countersuits, in "the law's delay" and the oblivion of old news. A year ago, two years, three, five—had I read this stuff? Had I remembered any of it? Not a line, not even the crucial fact that one of the indispensable legal minions who protracted and delayed was Max's dear friend, Herb Rosen. His name came swimming up from a mess of type with a bite like a piranha. I'd always been indifferent to Herb, ignoring his triumphs and his cases, and I hadn't bothered to keep track. But he'd defended UB in several actions and had represented Tomco at least once—in a dispute with the Teamsters. I was thinking over the implications when Wolfe reappeared. He leaned over the table, lean as a crane, and deposited another file. "Any luck?"

"Yes and no," I said. "It's amazing no one asked questions about these two outfits before."

"You can ask," Chester said. "The public doesn't always answer."

"Yes, that's true. What surprised me is that Herb Rosen defended in several of the cases."

"No surprise. He's one of the biggest lawyers in the state."

"He was Max's lawyer. He's my children's trustee. And he handled my ex-husband's literary deals. Do you see the problem?"

"I do, indeed! This is very interesting, and there's another angle. Rosen undoubtedly introduced Max to the Salisburys. And probably promoted the idea for the book, not knowing the sort of book Max would produce."

"Why do you say that?"

Chester Wolfe nodded sagely. "Herb Rosen's the insiders' bet for the Salisbury campaign. If there is one."

"State chairman, you mean? Herb Rosen?"

"You're surprised?"

"I knew he'd been active in the party—" I felt a little ill and must have looked it, because Chester said, "That's bad news?"

"I'm not sure." I didn't know what to think. The shortlist for Max's death kept increasing. But I didn't want to talk to Wolfe about that. "I guess I'd have to ask the senator."

"The senator's mind isn't on politics at the moment."

"No?"

"You can't have seen the paper this morning." He went over to the counter and picked up a copy. "Society bash—supposedly raising awareness of the need for historic preservation. Actually a thank-you for some big spenders."

The paper's Living Section detailed plans for the party's centerpiece—a professionally staged, fully costumed Thirties Murder Mystery Night. The producer of this quasi-theatrical entertainment had been interviewed about the elaborate props and costumes and about the plot, which was designed to utilize all the main public rooms of the newly restored mansion. The wonders of the latter were elaborated in an accompanying story, touting both its authenticity and opulence.

"Sounds like Versailles," I said. "Is this man really a member of Congress?"

Chester laughed. "Until he ascends higher."

"It'll need to be a mighty big throne. When is this extravaganza?"

"Tomorrow."

"Perhaps I'll drop in. I could come as that curiosity—a member of the public."

"I wouldn't try that," Chester said. "It'll be security like Fort Knox."

"No press?"

"Only the parties maven." He tapped the byline on the story. "The rest of us—no way. This is to be strictly nonpolitical."

"So they say." I smiled, but realized that Chester Wolfe wasn't joking.

"The story's bound to break," he said.

"I want it to break. I'm sure you see how important it is—for me and for the children. We now have an alternative to depression, murder, suicide. It's not an open-and-shut case anymore."

"The case has already been closed."

"I intend to reopen it. I'm convinced this material—" I patted the manuscript and the file folders—"will put pressure on the police. I'll give you copies of whatever you want. And the Australian's name and number, so you can check out that end. Plus whatever information I can give you—it's yours and you're welcome to it."

"You understand, my editor would prefer a human interest piece—a 'devoted widow seeks husband's vindication' sort of thing."

"A nauseating idea—and I'm not sure there's a concise term for ex-wife of the deceased."

"But you do understand," Chester Wolfe said, nodding his shaggy head for emphasis, "you do understand that the people involved are some serious trouble. When the story breaks, be careful. And before it breaks, be doubly careful."

I told him I intended to be, but I didn't feel careful. I felt optimistic: we were going to reopen the case and clear Max. He was finally going to get tidied up and out of my life for good. Yes, "optimistic" is the word, not "crazy." I never intended to be crazy, it just developed over time, and once the craziness was full-blown, there wasn't much I could do but go along with it.

Moira was gone when I got back in the afternoon. I really couldn't blame her for not wanting to stay around the place alone. Skipper was barking out of sheer boredom, and I brought him into the house and promised him a walk. I was getting ready to take him when Detective Crombie rang. I started to tell him about the slugs and the manuscript, but I could tell that his mind was on other things.

"Warren Landis," he said.

I waited.

"Warren Landis was found dead today near the river."

It shouldn't have been a shock, but it was.

"What happened?" I asked, but I wasn't thinking stroke or heart attack or even alcoholic collapse.

"He'd been shot in the head."

"The hiker," I said. "What about him? Was that really just a head injury from a fall?"

"No," Crombie said. "But that's not for public consumption."

"I see."

"We're pretty sure he was the one who killed your livestock. I shouldn't think you'd have to worry too much now."

"You're kidding," I said. "Someone means business. First Max and Bev and her boy, and now Landis. I want protection for my kids. You know where they are."

There was a pause, then he said he'd see what he could arrange. I hung up, feeling terminally nervous. Skipper jumped around my feet and leaned against my legs until I snapped on his leash and took him to the field. Warren Landis was dead! Warren Landis, the trucker who'd worked for Tomco, who'd been married to Bev, who had, maybe, broken up our farm and brought us to the verge of bankruptcy. Warren Landis might have gone crazy with grief, but I didn't see him as capable of killing his son. In fact—but I never finished that thought, because from the field I could see the road, and on the road, near one of the telephone poles, was a dark Taurus wagon with heavily tinted windows. I'd been having trouble with the phone. I'd had trouble calling Crombie—correct that, I'd gotten nothing but a busy signal. And calling the paper that morning—I'd given up and taken a chance on catching Wolfe. I didn't like the implications at all. The farm is quite isolated, and once the school traffic and the few commuters pass, the road is dead quiet.

"Come on, Skipper," I said. I wanted to get back to the house, to good solid old-fashioned doors and Sam's .22. I'm not sure what I planned to do, but my mind was made up for me by the phone. I heard it go onto the answering machine as I opened the door. The machine was burbling that "Alice and Moira are out but will be pleased to return your call," and behind it I heard Julie's voice.

"Mom . . ." Her words were lost in instructions to "leave your message after the beep."

"Dear, I'm downstairs. I can't turn it off. What's up?"

"Mom, Doug saw that man."

"What man?"

"He says the one in—" The hoot from the answering machine cut us off.

"Where?" But I could feel my anxiety rising to a whole other level.

"In the forest that time. He said to tell you the man with the tattoo."

"Where did he see him?"

"Here. In the restaurant. He came in, Mom. Doug cleared the table."

"God! Did he see your brother?"

"Yeah, but he didn't recognize him. Doug doesn't think."

"When was this?" I looked at the clock. It was after five.

"He's here now. He was here. Maybe he's gone by now. They were finishing up."

"How was he dressed? Trucker's cap, windbreaker?"

"No. Dark suit. Doug wasn't sure until he saw the tattoo. What are we going to do, Mom?"

"You're going to get his license number if you can, and you're going to call the police. I'll give you the number. Tell them exactly what you've told me, then stay out of sight."

"Can't you call, Mom?" She was nervous.

"It'll be better coming from you. Trust me. I'll call you later. If for any reason you can't get me, phone Sam. All right, dear? And for God's sake, be careful!"

I put down the phone, wondering if I'd done the right thing, if I should have driven to the shore and gotten them on a plane. But the dark car was still sitting on the road, and instead of being sensible, I went crazy. That's the only explanation. I grabbed some nylons, a dress, and heels—not

too high, but a bit awkward for all that. Put my good watch—
a nice one with small diamonds, a last anniversary present
from Max—in my pocket along with a comb. The sky looked
dull, as if it might rain, and I hauled out my good dark taffeta
raincoat—another relic of fancy evenings and other lives. I
put my license, my car keys, and a few dollars for gas in the
small beaded purse that I used to take to the opera. Then I
switched on the kitchen radio good and loud and put on
some lights. I bundled up the clothes, slid the clip in Sam's
.22, and loaded clothes, .22, and manuscript into the Honda.
I was seriously tempted by the truck, but it was parked at
the front of the yard, visible from the road; I'd just have to
risk the Honda's undercarriage. Skipper danced back and
forth, sensing something was up, and I got his long leash
and put him in the car. Then I went back inside and ran
upstairs to Doug's window. The Taurus was still sitting at
the side of the road. So far so good. I locked the house and
went out to the car.

The Honda can be cranky, and it starts with a roar. I kept
my eyes on the rearview mirror, which reflected the innocent
driveway and the pasture across the road. I slipped into gear,
made the tight turn by the barn, and pulled across the soft
track by the garden. Thank God it had been dry the last few
days. I stopped at the barred gate to the pasture, removed
the last pole, then pulled through. The little car bounced
onto the wagon track, the long weeds slapping at the undercarriage and clicking against the sides. Over the top of the
hill, around the glacial rock—too large for even the colonists'
oxen to move, down the other side.

We skidded once on loose gravel, but the wheels held. I
stopped at Mawson's pasture, opened the gate and drove
through, surprising a group of his young Herefords, who
jumped away clownish and stiff-legged. I glanced nervously
behind me, but the hill was empty, and the owners of the
Taurus were not risking its muffler and tailpipe. I rolled
across the pasture, unbarred the gate on the other side, and
pulled into the Mawsons' barnyard. I was relieved to find
that the truck was out, and Daisy's Toyota nowhere to be

seen. I really didn't want to have to explain what I was doing
sneaking out the back way with Skipper, a .22, and a bundle
of evening clothes. The Mawsons' young collie bitch was tied
up in the back. She and Skipper were good buddies, and I
didn't think she'd mind if I snapped Skipper's leash to her
line. I gave both dogs a pat, then got myself and the Honda
out of the yard and onto the state road as fast as its four
cylinders could take us.

At the McDonald's in the next town, I found a public
phone and dialed Herb Rosen's office.

"Attorney Rosen is just leaving for the day."

"This is Alice Bertram. I've got to talk to him—just for a
minute. He's expecting my call."

She huffed and grumbled for a minute, then Herb came
on the line. "Alice, I'm on my way home."

"I'll meet you there. I've got to see you."

"Can't it wait until tomorrow?"

"No. I've got to see you tonight."

"No can do. Jessie and I have to go out."

"The big Salisbury party, I assume."

"Yes."

"That's a late start. I can be in town"—I checked the
clock—"by seven." He started to protest. "It'll only take a
minute. Literally."

"Can't this be done over the phone, Alice?" His voice min-
gled exasperation and apprehension in roughly equal amounts.

"I'll see you at seven," I said.

I changed in the ladies room, struggling into nylons and
heels and combing my hair. I'd forgotten a lipstick but remembered a comb, and when I was as presentable as possible, I put on my good watch and rolled my slacks and shirt
in a bundle around my sneakers. At the door, I checked the
parking lot: no dark Taurus. No dark cars at all. It was six-
fifteen, and with most of the traffic outbound I made good
time. I rolled into the outskirts of Herb's very exclusive suburb as the last of the high-pressure executive class were
straggling home in their big cars with tinted glass and phone
antennas. It had started to rain, and I was pleased that I'd

thought of the raincoat: concentrate on trifles if you're going
to be crazy, is my advice. Herb's street was well lighted;
otherwise, it was what a country lane would be if it came
into money, a stretch of smooth, winding curves, lined with
expensive evergreens and blooming shrubs, mason-built
stone walls, decorative gates and pillars, and big carriage
lights. The houses were set far apart on well-treed lots, and
despite the streetlights, the area was dark and mysteriously
shadowed, with only the city shine to give away the fact that
this was strictly domesticated and picturesque *haute sub-
urbe*. Herb's house was one of the biggest and best, a handsome English-style brick, with a fine terrace and a king's
ransom of shrubbery. The lights on the driveway were all on,
for the lord and lady of the manse were about to go out for
the evening; the big Mercedes waited at the door, smooth as
a hunk of black jade.

I rang the bell. One of the good-looking boys in Herb's
photos answered the bell. Jason, last seen at seven. Or was
it eleven? "Oh, hello, Mrs. Bertram. Mom and Dad are just
getting ready to go out."

"I know. I just need to see your father for a minute. I'll
wait here."

"Okay. Dad! Dad, Mrs. Bertram's here!"

I heard Herb's voice from the upper reaches and smiled at
his son.

"He'll be down in a minute," the boy said, and disappeared
toward the sounds of a television set and adolescent voices.

"Fine." I smiled again—it's a sign of craziness—and
looked around the foyer, which was all white and gold, with
good antique prints in overly ornate frames. There was a nice
little gilded hall table, one of those cut-in-half jobs designed
to sit against a wall out of the way. On it was a stiff, creamy
envelope embossed with the Salisburys' address, which disappeared into my raincoat pocket just before Herb came
down the big curving staircase. His bowtie was undone, and
he was fiddling with his cuff links.

"Really, this is not the time, Alice," he said by way of
greeting.

"I'll only take a minute. You may want your raincoat."

"Raincoat?"

"It's drizzling. There's something in my car."

"What?"

"It came today. I thought you should see it. Part of that manuscript. I really think you should have a look . . ." I babbled on until he followed me out the door and over to the Honda. Fortunately, the rain had intensified, and when I said, "Just get in the front for a moment," he opened the door and sat down in the driver's seat. I went around to the trunk for the .22. Holding it in a fold of my raincoat, I opened the passenger's door, climbed past the seat, and sat down in the back.

"Can you close the door, Herb?"

"Alice, what the hell is going on?"

I waited until he'd shut the door, then handed him the keys. "These are the keys, Herb, and this is a loaded rifle. Start the car."

Herb has been in hundreds of court cases, and I was afraid he might recognize a bluff. But he looked at the gun, looked at me, and put the keys in the ignition.

"I'm going to drive this downtown to the police station, Alice. You'd better have a good story."

"Oh, I do, Herb. But don't turn toward downtown." I bit my lip and rested the barrel of the rifle against his ear. "We're going out to Senator Salisbury's party. Take a left here."

"You'll lose the children with this stunt."

"And you can lose yours, Herb, if you don't drive carefully."

"You wouldn't do it, Alice."

"Well, that depends, doesn't it? You went to some effort to make me out to be a crazy lady, didn't you, Herb? How ironic if you were right after all. 'Poor Alice. You know Max gave her an awful time. No surprise really that she got a little peculiar, a little obsessive.' Am I right, Herb? A word to the wise? A little hint—and so convincing coming from the family lawyer! I imagine Detective Crombie appreciated the background information. I was too stupid to see that. It's a mistake to be paranoid, even a feminist paranoid. I took it personally; I took it as part of the system, instead of looking for reasons why a nice, conscientious officer thought I was a loonie."

Herb hesitated at the light, but turned, not toward the station but toward the highway.

"You ought to signal turns, Herb."

"You know this is crazy, Alice. You know that."

"What you've been saying all along, Herb."

"I'm not taking you to the Salisburys'. Listen, we'll talk, Alice, all right? Drive around a bit and talk?"

"Fine. Let's talk first about Detective Crombie. The Simmons kidnapping? You represented the family in that case. He was in charge of the investigation. It was just wrapping up when Max and Bev and her boy were found. Is that right?"

"About right."

"And you'd had lots of chances to talk to Crombie, who's a personable guy. They tell me you're one of the very best, Herb. Good reputation, in spite, I must say, of having some dubious clients. What could be more natural? A passing comment, an aside. A 'Sorry you've got the Bertram case. Alice will give you all you can handle.' Something like that?"

"Alice, you had all those crazy notions. You don't remember the state you were in."

"Not that way, Herb," I said as he slowed near an exit. "We're going northeast."

"What'll you do if I turn this car around?"

"I don't know, Herb. I might shoot you, and unlike poor Max, I won't miss. I'm in a very bad way, and I'm scared for the kids, and I just might do it. On the other hand, I might not. I might let you drive to the station and tell them everything."

I thought I saw his shoulders stiffen.

"And what would you tell, Alice?"

"That you were Max's oldest friend and his literary agent and adviser. That in this case you had a serious conflict of interest, which Max perhaps—no, certainly—knew about, because I think he did try to keep the pertinent parts of the manuscript from you. That, nonetheless, you found out about it. And betrayed him, Herb."

"That's goddamn nonsense. Why the hell would I do that to my oldest friend?"

"Because Max was going to compromise your man, and then bye-bye state chairmanship. But I'd do you justice, Herb, I don't think that was the reason. The real reason was that Max was screwing around with your daughter Diana."

The car gave a violent swerve, then Herb stepped on the gas.

"I can prove that," I said, ignoring the fact that the over-taxed Honda was beginning to shudder. "The only question is whether you killed him or whether you talked to the people who did."

"That's all supposition and nonsense."

"You mean I don't have proof?"

"Not a shred. And all the forensic evidence is against you."

"Not all. Something new has turned up. And there's proof as far as Diana is concerned. He was seen with her. There's no doubt."

"Goddamn him. He deserved it! Why the hell didn't you stay with him, Alice?"

"Because then I might have done him in."

He looked up in the mirror, a quick, frightened look. He wasn't sure, after all. "You didn't, Alice. Did you?"

"No. I almost did once. You didn't know about that, I guess, since the divorce was amicable. I'm quite innocent—unless you really think I'm crazy. In a sense, it's up to you."

"Listen, Alice, the verdict was the best way. For all concerned."

"That's a matter of debate, isn't it? Better for your important friends, better for you, better, perhaps, for Diana—but not much better. Not better for me and the kids and Max's parents."

"And reopening all this—that's going to help? Involving other families, other people?"

"Other people have to pay their share of the freight.
Friends of your friends have about ruined me."

"They'll pay," Herb said quickly. "You know they'll pay."

"Did they offer to pay Max? Did he refuse—or didn't he
have a chance?"

Herb swerved off onto an exit ramp without speaking.
When we were on the secondary road, he said, "Diana's just
seventeen."

"Yes, I know."

"I'd known Max—how long, Alice? Twenty years?"

"At least."

"You see what I'm saying?"

"Yes."

"I don't understand him. You understand him?"

"Max liked sex, and he liked danger. Until very recently,
sex had stopped being dangerous. Once he could have been
fired for flirting with a student, compromised for making
eyes at a faculty wife. Max should have lived in the eighteenth century."

"I think he was a bastard," Herb said.

"So was it you, Herb? Were you the one?"

"No! I was as shocked as you. That's true, Alice."

"Then who was it? One of Salisbury's people? Someone
who works for the Forgettes? Or Tomco Trucking—my personal hunch?"

"I don't know," said Herb.

"Come on! You're the lawyer. You're the one who knows
the criminal element. You must have a guess."

"I never wanted to know," he said softly.

"Ah." I leaned back in the seat, the .22 cradled in my lap.
"You'll understand then why I have to meet these people? I
do want to know. And I think I'll find out tonight."

We were not very far from the Salisburys' place by this
time. The road was dark and winding, the occasional lights
far back in the trees.

"I don't want to be responsible, Alice."

"You're already responsible, Herb. For part of this. But
tonight's on me."

He found the drive, lit by two old-fashioned streetlights. "You won't get in," he said. "And Jessie will be worried. She'll call the police."

"I'm counting on her calling the police," I said.

There were security men checking the cars, reaching in to look at invitations.

"Roll down the window," I said, sticking the .22 out of sight under the seat. "And give the man our invitation."

Chapter 15

Herb parked between a BMW and a Cadillac. The left front door of the Honda is cranky, and he had to slam it several times before it shut. "I don't know why you don't drive a decent car, Alice."

"I don't have a decent income, Herb. Besides, it's good for you to see how the rest of us live."

He gave me a sour look. "At least you're dressed for this."

"I thought that might have tipped you off. But you're unobservant for a lawyer. Not very Rumpole."

"I don't know how you can joke," he said, peering into the back, looking for the rifle.

"I can joke because I'm crazy," I said. "Don't worry. It's out of sight."

"I should have security arrest you."

"On what grounds?"

"That weapon. Kidnapping. Threatening."

"It's safe in the car, and besides I came in with you. The rifle was a prop for the party—unneeded, but signals got crossed. Don't embarrass yourself." I took his arm and felt him recoil. "What I want is very simple. I want to meet the senator and Messieurs Tomcarelli and Forgette. That's all. You can pretend you've never met me." As I spoke, I caught one of my unaccustomed heels in the spongy grass and stumbled slightly, so that Herb had to hold me up.

"Be careful, Alice," he said.

Beyond the field and the gardens stood the big chateau, drawing enough power to deplete the Northeast grid. Every room was so brilliantly lit that the building seemed insubstantial, afloat in the misty air like Prospero's cloud-capp'd towers. The gardens were equipped with low, tasteful spotlights that turned the bedding plants to jewels, and the trees were strung with Japanese lanterns that had survived the brief downpour to glow through the leaves like the spirits of the blessed. Bands were playing: a rock beat pounded in the gardens while, within the house, saxophones led the way through Cole Porter and light Swing in honor of the evening's entertainment. Arriving guests were crunching over the gravel court, their voices like birds, their feet like insects, while on the drive, powerful motors hummed and an occasional walkie-talkie crackled.

"Welcome to the *ancien regime*," I said.

"Max used to call you Red Alice."

"You don't have to be Red Anything to see this as an invitation to revolution. This has passed comfort and reached ostentation."

"A monument to the taste of the Gilded Age," Herb said. "Part of our cultural heritage."

"Don't quote the PR to me, Herb. This is mob money, made from poisoning the rest of us. And you want to put this guy in the White House!"

"You've lived too long in the country," Herb said as we went up the marble steps to the main reception room. "This is the way things work."

"Tell me more. I'm thinking better of Max all the time. Thanks, I will," I said as a tray came by. It was a good domestic champagne, and I could feel it bubbling straight to my brain.

"Watch that stuff."

"You worry about all the wrong things," I said, and

stepped into the crowd milling about the great marble foyer.
Three stories above us—four in any normal scale—was an
immense coffered ceiling supported by limestone columns
and adorned by swags of carved stone and stucco, marble
panels, and gilded sculpture. Ranged below were the galleries
that ran along the upper floors, giving access to the bedrooms
and studies and all the hideaways and libraries and little
sitting rooms of a big private house. An enormous glass and
crystal chandelier hung from the center, and glass doors gave
out on the gardens and on a stone terrace, as crowded as the
foyer. "Where will the senator be?" I asked Herb.

He shrugged. "He'll come out and work the crowd for a
while. Then retreat upstairs with a few friends."

"And what did he know?" I asked. Herb's face was blurred
against the crowd, the lights, the refracted radiance of jewels,
the indoor fog of cigarettes. "Nothing, everything, something?"

"Something," he said. "I think something. But not much."

"There he is," I said, spotting the famous blond head, tall
above the crowd. "Introduce me, Herb."

"Alice . . ."

"More direct methods will get us both in trouble," I said.

The senator was preceded by a babble of greetings and con-
gratulations, by sighs of appreciation and admiration and good
wishes, by the laughs and shouts of those on the outskirts
pushing forward to be noticed. "Great party, Senator. Wonderful house, Senator. A masterful job of reconstruction! A
tour de force of decoration!" Greetings to his lovely wife, to
his family, to the senatorial pets, two- and four-legged. The
Honorable advanced through the throng like a demigod. By
rights he should have had a cape, a toga, a greatcoat, something that billowed, something baroque. He was big and
handsome in an overfed way, fair, ruddy-faced, full of smiles.
His voice was loud and hearty, spitting out names like a
computer. And there was a bland young aide beside him to
make introductions the instant it became clear that the great
man had forgotten a face. The senator moved like an idol on
wheels, smooth, unthinking, unstoppable, and shook Herb's

hand with sounds of recognition and delight. "And Mrs. Rosen?" He looked around, over my head.

"One of the kids," Herb said quickly. "One of those last-minute bugs."

"Give her my best," the senator said, ready to roll.

"This is Alice Bertram."

"My late husband, Max Bertram, wrote a book about your family, Senator Salisbury."

"Yes?" Serene disinterest.

"I would like to talk with you for a moment, if—"

"No business," said the aide smoothly. "This is a party."

"My husband wrote a book about the senator," I repeated softly, "and then he was murdered."

His eyes caught mine for an instant, before the shutters came down. "Come see us, Herb," the senator said. "And bring Jessie."

"Soon," said Herb.

The aide had taken my arm, a friendly, confidential gesture that said "old political friend," "old acquaintance." Where he would have taken me, I don't know, because just then there was a great shifting and exclaiming as a space was cleared to the front of the entryway. An old party dragon had sloshed her champagne in the excitement, and she said, "Oh, hell! Peter, get me a towel or something."

Peter released my arm immediately and whipped out a handkerchief.

"I'm getting too old for these stand-up affairs."

"Never say that, Mrs. Quinnet. Never say that!" He began sponging her acres of brocade, and I moved into the crowd as the actors came up the steps with the exaggerated voices and gestures that betray their profession. There were ten of them in thirties dress, led by a white-haired chap with a monocle—big and handsome and almost too like the senator—arm in arm with a splendid Margaret Dumont–style dowager. She was carrying a frightened looking ball of fluff and saying, "I do wish you'd reconsider, Reggie, dear."

"That young lout's a bounder. I'll be dashed. Do you know what he showed up at the club wearing? . . ."

Behind them came another pair, a young man and woman in old-style tennis dress, wooden, pre-Prince rackets in their hands. "But Daphne," the young man whined.

"Sorry, Biffer, Daddy's adamant."

"I thought he was cement."

"Fortune's cement, Daddy's adamant. And it's that kind of joke that's made him so. If you can't be sensible . . ."

The third couple were a youngish man in plus fours and his older companion, a fellow in a checked suit and loud sweater who was clearly not from the best of circles. They were arguing furiously about a gambling debt with recriminations on both sides. Next came a very thin woman with marcelled hair, a beaded dress, and a foot-long cigarette holder, accompanied by her male counterpart, a greyhound of a man dressed, like the first couple, in evening dress. "The will," the woman said, "you've got to keep your mind on the will, Bertie."

"Damned if he's going to tell me," the man said. "He'll up and change it."

"Not if he doesn't *know*, Bertie." Her high voice ricocheted off the plaster and stucco, off the coffers of the ceiling, off the gilt and trim.

Finishing the procession were a dignified butler, carrying a visiting card on a silver tray, and a perky looking chambermaid with an ostrich-feather duster. "I tell you, I seen that fellow, before. Yellow shoes and a purple tie!"

"Unsuitable even for a horse blanket," the butler remarked, his vowels flat, elongated, comically superior.

He was followed by a smattering of applause as the crowd trailed after the performers, some consulting their programs and identifying the characters; others seeking the drawing room where the next installment of the mystery would unfold. I went along and, catching a glimpse of the senator's aide in the crush, squeezed out of sight behind a decorative screen.

Ten minutes later, at the end of a highly charged scene between Mr. and Mrs. Bertie and the fellow with the gambling debts, the party oozed toward the morning room, and

I emerged to look around. The lavish and enormous drawing room was empty except for a few older revelers who'd found the overstuffed chairs and couches irresistible; the foyer, too, had been depleted, although there must have been a hundred guests in all, perhaps twice that number. The immense mansion and its dance floors devoured crowds, and I was thinking that the Salisburys' peripatetic entertainment made perfect sense, when my path crossed the sartorially outrageous gambler's. Close up, I recognized Fitzie Holmes, a drama student I knew. I waved and asked, "Can I say hello, or are you in character?"

"Hello, Alice. I'm not in character for"—he checked his watch—"twenty minutes. Actually, I don't have a big part. I'm your basic bad-influence role."

"I hope you're at least a suspect."

"Everyone's a suspect."

"Better than the victim."

"Short evening for victims," Fitzie agreed.

"Some set," I said, looking around. The corridor was marble and limestone, hung with decent nineteenth-century landscapes.

"Fabulous. Good for practicing one's concentration. The acoustics are weird."

"The crowd must help."

"Yes, thank God we've only got one scene upstairs. Fans watch from below on that one."

"What's upstairs like?"

"Like down. Not quite so overbearing, actually. The family quarters are quite modern."

"Where are they?" I asked, stretching my neck to look up at the galleries.

"Third floor. Other side. We had the full tour. Wonderful views. You can see the Sound in clear weather."

"Bit of a hike upstairs, though."

"Oh, there's an elevator on the other side of the hall. Well, I've a few props to collect. Good to see you, Alice." He headed in the general direction of the entertainment, and I moved with the guests drifting toward the bar set up in the formal dining room—"restored to its original splendor in crimson silk brocade and French paneling"—if I remembered correctly. Near the exit from the dining room, I spotted the elevator with a security guard loitering beside it. A quick canvass of the stairs told the same story. Downstairs we were welcome to revelry and historic restoration. Upstairs was strictly off limits.

I refilled my champagne glass to look festive and went out onto the terrace, a semicircle of flagstones with a flower-laden balustrade around the edge. Five or six feet below was a dance floor packed with the younger crowd, some of whom were lounging on the long stone stairs that led to the gardens. A variety of security personnel were disposed along the top landing, and when I looked over the edge, I saw why. There was a steep drop from the terrace to a rocky garden and a sunken drive that ran under the terrace for deliveries, I guessed, and to the various outbuildings. From the house and the stairs, one saw only the sweep of the gardens, spangled with lights and full of music. I walked down to the bottom of the steps and wandered along the gravel paths of the gardens. But though I saw other security personnel, caterers, and factotums, I did not see the man with the tattoo, nor the senator's aide, nor anyone who looked like the newspaper images of Bob Tomcarelli or Martin Forgette, and I returned to the house. There I consulted my program and sat down near the elevator. The actors arrived a few minutes later, the pretty young woman now out of tennis clothes and into a fawn evening costume. She was arguing with her young man, but broke off to "check on Daddy." She looked into an alcove that had been hidden until a few minutes earlier by a caterer's table and let out a bloodcurdling shriek. The guests came hurrying into the reception room, and mindful of the Chinese vases and Italian urns—and no doubt trained to investigate even theatrical screams—the security people moved slightly away from their posts toward the center of the room. I guessed that "Daddy" had turned up with his feet in cement, but did not stop to check. Instead, I reached for the elevator button, and when the door slid open, stepped inside. The door closed on the guard's surprised face.

It opened again on the upper floor, and luckily—or unluckily—for me, a group of actors were assembling on the floor below. The lights were suddenly doused, and several people ran heavily along the corridor. There was a shout, then a shot, monstrously loud, which resulted in exclamations of surprise, shock, and theatrical gratification, effectively drowning the electronic cackle of the walkie-talkies. I opened the first door I saw and got inside before the lights came up again.

I was in a bedroom big enough to hold a small cottage. The lights from the garden lit up the long mirrors, the crystal fixtures, the rows of prints and family photos. From the hall, I heard declamations and wails, accusations mingling with protests of innocence. I crossed the room quickly and went through the bathroom shared with the adjoining room. Curiously, and I would have thought, inconveniently, the Salisbury mansion had followed the old aristocratic plan of linked rooms. In the third one over, I heard voices, thought I recognized Herb's, and stopped. The shadows of the trees dappled the walls with a shifting pattern of light and dark, so that the pictures, furniture, and decorations blended into ambiguous patterns where nothing seemed as clear as it had before. The voices were muffled by the solid old construction, but I heard snatches.

". . . potentially a problem . . ."

". . . was all done . . . without consultation. I don't like that. We have to be . . ."

Then a voice, slightly higher, without accent or idiosyncrasy, as if it had been laundered to remove distinguishing marks: ". . . what had to be done. You understand, John. Certain things have to be accomplished and that means . . ."

It was the voice on the phone, colorless, and for that very reason a great stimulus to the imagination, especially when it was warning, threatening. It was warning now. Warning the senator, perhaps, or Herb. Next it would threaten, but perhaps it would tell me what I wanted to know, and though

I felt my heart pounding on my interior walls like an unwelcome tenant, I moved closer. I didn't hear anyone behind me until the rear door opened. I turned into the bright circle of a flashlight, then the overhead light came on. Peter, the senator's aide, had a green-tinged aura, and the high ceiling light revealed a walnut bedroom suite, striped paper, a French rug; the flashlight, a revolver, big trouble. I don't know what he had in mind, but I turned to the connecting door and knocked loudly. Peter swore and stepped forward, reaching for my arm, but the voices had already stopped and the door opened.

"Sorry, Senator," he said. "Minor problem."

"Who is it? No one's supposed to be up here."

"Alice Bertram. Our earlier conversation was interrupted, Senator." I wrenched my arm free and stepped past the man at the door into a richly paneled study. There were two dark leather chairs and a leather sofa arranged around a mahogany coffee table that held cut-crystal decanters and a large bowl of nuts and crackers. The senator was sitting with a look of nervous displeasure. His face seemed redder than I'd remembered, and as I came into the room, he took a quick sip of his drink. Herb was on the couch—called, no doubt, to account for the momentary unpleasantness in the reception room—and he looked paler than usual. The tall man who'd opened the door sat down next to him. This was Tomcarelli, I guessed. I remembered the handsome, heavy features from the news photos, but his chilly wet-marble eyes had escaped the photographer. In private, the socialite refuse magnate showed an old Roman face, hard and unimaginative.

The other chair, the power position, was held by Forgette. He was smaller than I'd have guessed from the press photos, a short, solid, well-balanced man with black hair, dark eyes, and a large, square, stubborn head. Considering the two of them, one would have said that Tomcarelli looked elegant and intelligent; Forgette, like a dressed-up stevedore. Appearances can be deceiving.

"I've been waiting to talk to you," I told the senator.

"This is a private meeting. Guests are not invited above the main floor. Peter, you'll call security."

"Right away," he said, but Forgette gave him a look, and he lingered by the door.

"I'm not sure that you know about all the things that are being done by your entourage. My husband—"

"Mrs. Bertram's ex-husband," Herb broke in. "Alice has taken his death very hard."

"Max Bertram murdered his live-in lover and her child, then shot himself," Forgette said. "The sort of tragedy your gun-control legislation would help to prevent." He looked at the senator as he spoke, sounding as if he were reading from a cue card.

"That is the official story," I said. "I have questioned it from the start. As a result, my business has been ruined, our livestock killed, and my children threatened."

"There has been some vandalism in Alice's area," Herb said.

"Rural areas are not immune to the scourge of drugs," Forgette replied sententiously.

"Nor senatorial circles, to thugs." He didn't turn a hair. "My husband had been commissioned to do a history of your family, Senator."

"No one authorized a biography," the senator said, suddenly alert. "There has been nothing officially authorized. There will be a campaign biography, certainly, but nothing has been finalized on that as yet."

"This was a history of your whole family, Senator, going back to the original settlers in the eighteenth century. I believe it was to be issued by the local historical society in connection with the reopening of this house."

"Oh, that," he said. "Some little thing Vivian was interested in. Family history. Nice historical anecdotes."

"My husband had his faults, Senator, but he was a good scholar. He did a thorough job—heavy on primary sources, letters, diaries, contemporary memoirs and accounts. Quite fascinating. When he came to the modern day, he was just as thorough. He apparently got interested in the project for its own sake and became curious about your sources of support, about your close ties with these two gentlemen, and about *their* business dealings."

"None of this has any bearing on the sad business of the Bertram killings."

"So one might think. But someone knew about the manuscript. Someone removed Max's notes and computer disks. The same someone, afraid that I had a copy, ransacked our house. And when the copy—which I didn't even know existed—didn't turn up, our small business was wrecked by someone who ran a truck through our gardens and killed our goats with a sledgehammer. Fortunately, none of us was at home. Had we been, we might have wound up like Max and Beverly and her son."

"Well, certainly we're very sorry, Mrs.—"

"Bertram," the aide said.

"—Bertram, but in no way does this concern us."

He used the imperial plural. Maybe it wasn't arrogance. He seemed very much the creature of his two associates, and perhaps it was a corporate "we," and his senatorial seat, a joint stock company.

"I think it does. In two ways. What the manuscript says about your business dealings is potentially damaging to your political future. That gives you—or one of your associates—a motive. Especially when United Biologicals and Tomco Trucking are under investigation for illegal toxic dumping. And then you—or one of your associates—knew about the manuscript long before I did, well before Max died."

"How's that?" the senator asked sharply.

"Herb knew. And had a reason to tell you. Or"—I looked around the room—"Mr. Forgette. Or Mr. Tomcarelli. What's more, Warren Landis may have known." The senator looked blank, and I said, "Bev Landis's estranged husband. A trucker with a violent temper, who sometimes drove for Tomco and who has just turned up dead."

"It had a bearing on the campaign," Herb said, and he might have said more if Forgette hadn't interrupted.

"These are very serious charges."

"It's a very serious situation. You have someone dangerous working for you—if what happened to Max was un-
planned, if things just got out of hand. Otherwise—"

"You have no proof," said Forgette.

"Proof comes in different forms. But you and I have talked
about this before, haven't we?"

"What's this about Martin?" the senator demanded.
"What the hell is going on here."

"I think Herb is right," Forgette said, getting to his feet.
"Mrs. Bertram is suffering from the aftereffects of traumatic
events. She forced her way in here after persuading Attorney
Rosen to bring her. Is 'persuade' the word, Herb?"

He had the grace to look uncomfortable. "There's a .22
in her car," he said.

"Ah. That gives us ammunition—no pun intended. But
we might not press charges if Mrs. Bertram is willing to stay
away from the senator and from the press."

"How much did the senator know?" I asked. "That will
be the question. And what else would you like to keep from
him?" I heard my voice rising and saw their faces closing
down. Men hold no stronger card than "female hysteria":
the more vehemently I protested, the easier they would find
it to ignore what I said. "You try charging me," I said to
Forgette, "and you'll have the kind of publicity you don't
want. Particularly if he's to be a presidential candidate. It
can't be done."

"No," said Tomcarelli. He had not spoken before. "Peter,
you better call Vic. You better see Mrs. Bertram safely out of
here."

"I don't like this," said the senator.

"Listen," said Herb, but no one did. Forgette was bending
the senator's ear, and Tomcarelli gave Peter a look.

"Come on, Mrs. Bertram." He grabbed my arm.

"Don't touch me," I said. "Or I'll start hollering."

Tomcarelli stood up, blocking the senator's view, and gave
me a push into the other room. "So scream," he said. "Part
of the theatrical entertainment." He gave a little laugh and
said, "Sometimes the senator is a genius."

"I think I'll give it a try anyway," I said, and I started to shout for help.

"Oh, shit!" Peter said. He began pushing buttons on his walkie-talkie and I made a break for the outer door. Mistake. Something hit the side of my head, and the room tilted sideways. I grabbed a bureau to keep from going over and swung a nice porcelain lamp, which connected with Tomcarelli's arm. I found a candlestick next and might have cleared off a fair portion of "the charming family mementoes that distinguish the Salisbury mansion" if a thick, strong arm had not appeared out of nowhere and wound itself like a boa constrictor around my neck while something very sharp took up lodging against my ribs.

"No more."

I nodded.

Tomcarelli disappeared back into the study with reassuring noises for the senator, and Peter put away his walkie-talkie and came over to take my arm. The man behind me relaxed his hold, and as he did so, the sleeve of his coat rode up. I saw the eagle tattoo, and a moment later the angry face I'd last seen in the state forest.

▽

Chapter 16

THEY TOOK ME INTO one of the bathrooms and locked the door. The ceiling was at least twelve feet high, which was relevant because there was no window, only a skylight. The floor was tile. The tub was an immense marble sarcophagus with clawed feet. The sink was an old-fashioned pedestal with brass fittings—very Victorian and in keeping with what the Salisbury decorator had referred to as the "high standard of finish and decoration." Only the toilet let down the standard. It was certainly not original, and whoever cleaned the bathroom had tended to skip around its base and to neglect an area just under the tub where several large spiders had set up shop. There was also chipped paint on the lower wall and some cracked plaster.

But these details should in no way reflect on the "luxurious ambiance" that readers of the daily paper had been assured characterized the "reborn Salisbury mansion." My reaction was colored by my unusual perspective. I was lying on the tiles halfway between the toilet and the sink. And had been for some time. Time that I seemed to have lost in the drunken stupor resulting from the bottle of vodka that Peter and his companion had poured down my throat. A fair bit had soaked into my clothing, more had wound up on the floor, where it was pooled like water after a careless shower,

but enough had wound up down my gullet to nearly knock
me out. Nearly—for it certainly had gotten to be three A.M.
in a hurry—but not completely. I've never been able to drink
vodka. My stomach recoils at the very thought of fermented
potatoes, and it had been recoiling in a vigorous way ever
since Peter said, "That's enough. Jesus, you don't want to
kill her, do you?"

And his friend with the tattoo and the knife and various
unarmed combat skills had said, "Not yet."

That's where I was at the moment. Half high and in deep
shit, with my brain spinning off on tangents. I studied the
pattern in the tile floor and pronounced it banal. Considered
the all-white decor and brought up, alternately, half-digested
alcohol and smatterings of the silliest newspaper stories. I
wasn't at all afraid. I wasn't at all concerned. The kids were
miles away; I was locked up in the most expensive house in
the county by the same folks who'd done Max in, and I
wasn't worried. I was thinking, instead, that given the way
I felt, death was probably underrated and that the Salisburys
could have matched their fixtures better. Then my stomach,
which seemed to have endless reserves, twitched again.

Some time after this, I realized that the bands, which had
played for so long they had become part of the background,
were silent. Somewhere musicians were packing up their
guitars and electric pianos, their saxophones, clarinets, and
drums, or were having a last smoke, a last drink—if they
were not already on their buses. My watch showed four in
the morning; the skylight had gone gray; the revelers had
gone home. I went over to the sink and splashed cold water
on my face. The security people would be leaving, and the
actors, the press. Probably, the senator and his charming
mate were going to bed, leaving the hour or so before dawn
for the night creatures on the staff. For the less-public personalities like the man with the tattoo.

At that thought, a memory swam from the alcoholic mists
like the Creature from the Black Lagoon: I'd told the man
with the tattoo. Whose name was Vic, whose personality
was homicidal. That was after we'd struggled. After I'd col-

lected the myriad bruises I felt along my back and shoulders.
After I'd stopped choking long enough to speak. "You're the
one," I'd said. "I'm sure it was you." Crazy woman: I was
lost, the children too, and even alcohol was no excuse for
such stupidity. But maybe someone was left. As I recalled,
Fitzie Holmes was a past master at procrastination. Or Herb.
Herb might have had second thoughts and pangs of guilt. I
stood up and shouted. The tiles reverberated like an echo
chamber, but there was not a sound from the neighboring
rooms or from the corridor. I picked up one of my shoes and
tried throwing it at the skylight. It hit the glass several times
without breaking a pane. I used the shoe next to hammer
on the door, which made a fine, unappreciated racket, then
turned my attention to the lock, which, like the handle, was
old and a bit loose but quite resistant.

I needed a hairpin, a nailfile, a convenient piece of metal,
but the bathroom was singularly ill equipped. I was trapped
until they came to let me out, and once they did, there'd be
no proof I was ever upstairs. If Jessie should later testify that
she'd been at the party, it would be her word against mine.
Inspired by this thought, I made an inventory of my possessions: Max's gift watch with my initials was the best bet. I
peeled off my pantyhose, dropped the watch into one of the
feet, and tied the whole affair around one of the dusty legs
of the tub, an effort that made me dizzy. Then I lay down on
the floor, where, some time later, I felt, more than heard, the
approach of footsteps. My first impulse was to get up and
make a lot of noise. My second was to feign unconscious-
ness. Someone touched the handle and I closed my eyes as
the door opened.

"Out cold," said a voice I recognized as Peter's, the
senator's aide. Curious duties Peter drew.

"I thought I heard her." That was Vic. With the tattoo
and the high-powered rifle.

"Doesn't look like it." He knelt down and took my wrist.
His hands were clammy. Peter was nervous, almost as nervous as I was.

"Don't worry. She's still alive."

"You can get alcohol poisoning," the aide said. He probably had all the statistics and anecdotes.

"Yeah. So they say. Help me get her on her feet."

They hauled on my arms, and I let my eyes open a fraction.

"Get the fucking shoes, will ya? You want to leave them here?"

Peter slipped them on my feet. I'd have to drop them somewhere; they were a menace on the soft grass and marble floors. "All right, let's go. I'll call security. Tell them we found her drunk in one of the rooms. That's the best we can do."

"Yeah. But don't call them, huh? Be smart. Go down to the main gate, will ya? Talk to Mike about it. Mike's the pro."

"Can you manage?" I could hear the relief in his voice. Peter's disease was only virulent Potomac fever; he really didn't want to be involved with anything else.

"Sure. What's your worry?" Vic suffered from another, more lethal, mania.

"We don't want any more trouble. Especially not here. The senator will be very unhappy if there's trouble around here."

"It's not the senator's neck, though, is it?"

"Forget that. She was out-of-her-mind drunk. Still is."

"*In vino veritas*, sucker. They teach you that at Yale?"

"She was scared to death."

"She's a crazy lady, as crazy as the other one. You weren't so squeamish about that, were you?" He mimicked a finicky voice, " 'Something has to be done soon, Vic. Something has to be done.' That was a different story, wasn't it?"

"She got greedy, and between the two of them she knew too much. That was different, you know that, Vic. Though you went too far."

"I did it so there was no questions. Right? No witnesses, no questions. Then this cunt comes nosing around. She's the kind that gives you nothing but trouble. Now you go down and talk to Mike. Which is the kind of errand you're good at, Peter."

"Vic, I don't know."

"Be smart. You don't want to know," Vic said and kicked open the door to the corridor.

The immense reception area had a stale, party breath—
the residue of too many cigarettes, spilled drinks, and expensive perfumes. In the dim light, the coffered ceiling pulsed
with decoration, the carved blocks moving in and out, the
stone swags on the walls swaying gently. I lurched and found
my feet and stopped.

"Come on, damn it."

We were near the wide stone railing. It was waist high and
wobbling. I put one hand out and shook my head. He glanced
around, then took a step closer.

"No," I said. It came out a scream. Whatever intellectual
resources had been dampened down by alcohol, the instinct
for self-preservation was quite intact. He clamped his hand
across my mouth, and I struggled ineffectually as he hauled
me toward the stair. I caught the railing and held on, but
clearly Vic's orders were to get me out of the house, because
he first tried to wrestle me away from the rail, then, that
failing, simply dragged me along, the smooth marble hand-
rail squeaking under my wet palm. Vic muttered under his
breath, his eyes wild. On the ground floor, I went limp, which
seemed like a good idea, since he then needed both hands to
pick me up. I got in another shout before he caught on and
got us both out the door.

Cool, damp night air hit me and, with it, comprehension.
Straight ahead was the edge of the terrace, high enough for
an inebriated guest who'd eluded security precautions to fall
to her death. There was a drive beneath. If the inebriated
guest survived, she could suffer misfortune from an early-
morning truck. I struggled to my feet and tried again to
disengage my rubbery arms and legs, but Vic was too strong.
Inexorably he began to draw me toward the edge, and time,
which had been lollygagging all evening, now took a giant
step and landed me at the railing. I kicked out and elbowed
Vic in the ribs, half strangling myself against his arm in the
process. He tried to pick me up bodily, but I'd recovered
enough to prevent that and in the struggle, neither of us
heard the door of the house open.

"What's going on?"

I twisted my head and shouted.

"Who's there? What's happening?"

Herb's voice, then the sound of running feet.

"Stop," he cried and touched Vic's shoulder.

Vic struck him so hard that he wound up against one of the big stone flower pots, and I took advantage of this loss of temper to wrench myself free. I got to the stair, stumbled, kicked off my shoes, and ran barefoot down the stone steps. There was a scuffle above, before I heard a clatter. I ducked around the corner, jumped into the sunken road, and ran back across the drive to the house. I tried the service door, which was locked, and found that the ground floor windows all had handsome old iron grilles. The gardens on my right were relatively open, but the road ran through a grove of trees toward some outbuildings, and hearing the rattle of loose stone behind me, I chose the barns.

I used to be quite a good runner, but that was years ago. Amend that to years and years. By the time I reached the trees, my lungs were rebelling, and I could hear Vic pounding after me on the road. With an effort, I reached a little shed at the edge of a wide, graveled yard. There were garages on the left side, stables on the right, sheds and barns directly opposite. Everything was dark except for a small light on the garage, and I froze behind a container of sand. I was afraid that Vic might check the shed, but he had apparently lost me in the darkness. He ran into the center of the yard, his feet noisy on the stones, and ran his flashlight over the fronts of the buildings. I ducked my head and waited. Vic started toward the open main door of the stable, and I thought that I would return the way I'd come, try the house again, find my car. I was edging back softly in the darkness, feeling for branches, for anything that might make a sound, when I felt a sharp pain in my left foot. I caught my breath in surprise. Out on the gravel, Vic turned his head and swung the flashlight. I made a dash from the blinding glare toward the far side of the stable, the beam brightening the ground in splashes around me. As I turned the corner, I heard him cutting through the center of the building, disturbing the horses with his rush, and changed direction toward the faint whitish outline of a cluster of greenhouses. The door of the first house was unlocked, and I opened it to the familiar smells of earth, damp wood, and fertilizer mingling with a light odor of insecticide and carnations. I heard Vic running, then the glass overhead shattered, and crouched behind the central benches, I scuttled through the connecting door to the next house, which was warmer and damper, full of tender tropicals. Vic reached the house behind me and switched the lights on. I ran down the duckboards to the wooden building beyond and wrenched open the door to the potting shed. I found the workbench and ran my hands frantically over its surface: heavy terra cotta pots, a dibble, reasonably sharp, a trowel, sharper. The light went on in the next house. I dropped to my knees, felt a watering can, a coil of hose. I heard a thud from the adjoining greenhouse and an exclamation of anger, as Vic bumped into one of the overcrowded benches. I almost got to my feet, but it had to be here somewhere, because I could smell— Then I touched a plastic canister with a spray attachment, lifted it, felt the weight, fumbled for the pump, and realized that it was a new, nonpriming model. The door to the potting shed banged open, light speared into the room, and I depressed the lever and aimed the spray at the door. A burst of sweetish poison filled the air and a handgun discharged, shattering pots, before the weapon rattled to the floor. Vic was shouting, his hands over his eyes. I hurled the heavy sprayer at his head and bolted.

Immediately outside were a double row of cold frames and a gravel path that led away in the graying morning to a large vegetable garden and open fields. I started toward the garden, limping heavily, but the gravel paths on my sore foot were excruciating; I'd never make it. I heard Vic thrashing around in the greenhouse and headed for the farm yard as fast as I could. By the time I reached the stable, I could no longer run, and I ducked inside. The horses wickered softly and stirred their feet uneasily as I passed their stalls. At the end, a second corridor led to storage areas and to a small tack room, saturated with the smell of leather and saddle soap. I was beginning to feel dizzy and a bit sick. I sat down with my head between my knees and saw a trail of dark splotches on the wood floor. I stuck my finger in one, felt the stickiness, and belatedly thought to look at my foot: the gaping cut that ran clear across the heel was bleeding profusely—and laying down a perfect trail.

I jumped up, forgetting the pain, and ran to the door. The front was inexplicably locked. I ran to the other end of the corridor and out the back. In front of me was a large manure pile with a pitchfork in it and a small fenced paddock. I had started between them, heading for the barns, when I heard footsteps in the stable. Vic came out the door, a flashlight in one hand, something that glittered in the other. I took a step backward toward the fork.

"Stop right there," he said.

I backed up another step, and as he made a grab for me, I seized the fork and swung it sideways against him, catching him off balance. Then I dodged back and pointed the tines at his chest. "Don't!" I yelled. "Don't come—"

But he dropped the light and raised his arm and lunged. I can't tell you how many loads of manure and compost I've shifted since we started the garden, but this old peasant weapon is as familiar to me as a rolling pin. I put all my weight behind the thrust and heard him scream as the prongs caught his arm and shoulder. I felt blood on my hands and tried to push him back. Then he was on the ground, the fork in the air, and there were voices, shouts.

"Here!" I called. "Here! We need a doctor."

Vic writhed on the ground. I saw the knife and tried to kick it away. His hand caught my bare foot before there was a roar of sound that set the horses whinnying and kicking their stalls in panic. Lights went on in the stable block, and the garage and the yard lit up like a stage set. In front of me was a great deal of blood and very little of Vic's head. My legs lost their bones, and I sat down on the damp, mucky ground, wiping bits of him off my face.

"Mrs. Bertram?"

Legs, a shadow, a hand reaching down for the knife, a bright reflection running off the blade.

"Mrs. Bertram?" It was Forgette.

"You killed him," I said. "In cold blood."

"He murdered your husband. Which was bad luck for him," he added, still in that calm, inflectionless, almost reflective tone. "We could have handled him."

"You were never after Max," I said, suddenly comprehending the bits and pieces I'd heard earlier. "He wasn't the target, it was Bev."

"Very clever, if a bit belated, Mrs. Bertram."

"She was blackmailing you—or Tomcarelli?"

"Both, actually. Not a lady with a sense of proportion."

"She put together what she knew from Max and what she knew from her husband."

"That's right. A risky business. Considering the personalities involved. And now she's dead along with your husband and Warren, and Vic"—he touched the body with one careless toe—"who also lacked a sense of proportion, was going to have killed you too." The knife was in his hand.

"They'll know I was here. I left—"

He stopped, momentarily uncertain. "What did you leave, Mrs. Bertram?"

"Max's watch. It's engraved. It'll be found."

"By me," he said and took a step.

I could hear a car, a siren, and I reached out to the manure pile, scooped up a handful of straw and dung, and threw it in his face. When Forgette raised his hands to wipe off the mess, I scrambled up and ran past the stable into the disorienting and hallucinatory lights of two squad cars.

"Catch her," someone said. "She's been shot."

"No," I said. "I'm all right. But he has a gun. Be careful."

One of the troopers put his hands on my shoulder. There were shouted questions, orders. The car radio crackled and squawked, then Forgette walked calmly through the stable arch, the revolver and the knife in his hands, and held them out to the troopers. I could hear his voice, low, reassuring, the voice of male rationality, and I said, "Look on the third floor. You'll see. And ask Herb Rosen. He knows." Then I felt the pulsing lights dim, the voices fade; I leaned against the car.

"An ambulance is on the way," one of the troopers said.

But a familiar truck was pulling into the yard and coming to a stop with a spatter of gravel. I could see that clearly.

"No," I said. "I just need some stitches. I'm going with Sam."

$\triangledown$

Chapter 17

I TOOK THE KIDS for a picnic at the shore a few days later—our first family outing since Max's death. Doug played on the rocks and threw stones in the water as if he were ten instead of thirteen, and Julie scrambled after him. I kept my wounded foot out of the sand with plastic bags and hobbled about with a cane. The night of the Salisbury party and the subsequent press seemed to have cleared our heads. Max might never get a complete public vindication, but we'd created a doubt, and the presumption of innocence was again on our side. That was important, particularly for the children, who began to show the signs of normal, rather than abnormal, grief. I found Julie crying in her room one afternoon and sat down and talked with her about Max. Doug asked if he could have his dad's gold watch—my son's more subtle way of saying that he was coming to terms. Things might still be rocky, but I thought that the kids would eventually be okay, and a week after the party I was feeling chipper enough to visit Herb Rosen.

I picked the day that Jessie had her League of Women Voters meeting and a time when the kids were in school. Sam drove me; my foot was pretty well healed, but he'd said he had to go into Hartford anyway, and I didn't like to refuse. He had been both more affectionate and more wary since the night at the Salisburys', when we'd wound up in a shouting match in the parking lot—a consequence of his .22, the kids' panic, and my less than optimal state. I hadn't taken that too seriously, however, and he'd been very kind at the hospital and ever since. Doug and Julie rated him highly, which pleased me more than the implication that while Sam was rock solid, I was somehow unpredictable, almost, but not quite, unreliable. You can see how much maternal devotion is taken for granted. Moira says that's reality and an important part of their development; I'm not sure Moira knows what she's talking about.

Herb's big house was quiet when we arrived, and Sam handed out the pots with a nice lemon thyme and a purple sage, trimmed up to look decorative.

"Do you want to meet Herb?"

"No, I'll take a walk," he said. We'd stopped at the McDonald's on the way in, and he'd provisioned himself with a cup of coffee.

"I won't be long."

"Take your time. I'm interested in the way they've vented this place." He pointed to the pipes in the steep roof.

"All right," I said, half relieved. I'm not sure that Sam and Herb would have hit it off.

As I came up the steps, Herb opened the door. His left arm was in a sling and his injured shoulder was still taped.

"For the gourmet cook," I said.

"Jessie will like those. If you could put them in the kitchen, Alice."

"Sure. How's the arm?"

"Sore. The shoulder is broken. Jessie'll be sorry she missed you."

"I guessed I was on her list at the moment."

"Well, maybe better this way. Shall we sit here? I'll heat up some coffee," he said, pushing a button on one of his space-age appliances. "How are the children, Alice?"

"You know kids—glad to be home and already missing life at Steak and Sprouts. But they'll be all right, I think. Now that the excitement's over."

"They're good kids," he said. "You should be thankful they were so persistent the other night with the police."

"I am. To them and Sam—and to you, Herb. I'd have been an 'unfortunate accident' except for you."

"I warned you not to have anything to do with that outfit."

"But I had to—I hope you see that."

He leaned against the counter and studied his manicured yard. "You've never mentioned Diana."

"I haven't had to. And I don't think she'll come up. The police seem to think that there were a lot of ways the Salisbury circle could have found out about the more sensitive portions of the book. Besides, it didn't take genius to guess where Bev Landis was getting at least half of her info."

"I'm grateful, Alice."

"How has Diana taken all this?"

"Hard. We have her seeing a therapist. Her mother doesn't know about Max," he added quickly.

"And now?"

"Maybe better."

"Max was a lecher, not a killer," I said.

"It puts things in perspective."

"Children are what put things in perspective."

"Yes. For you alone, Alice, I'm frankly not so sure," he said. "But I didn't want your kids left."

"Fair enough," I said. "Just for you, I'd probably have told everything. For Diana and your family, I'm keeping quiet. Clearing Max is enough."

He surprised me and laughed. "We're too much alike, Alice, that's our trouble. No, don't look around like that. Back to the soil's your style, just as this is mine."

"There may be something in that."

"What about money? Is that going to be all right?"

"I think so. There's quite a bit of interest in the book."

"That's strictly long-term finance."

"Don't I know it. Moira and I have decided to sell most of the farm. I hate to do it, but it's just beyond us. We think the fellow who rents the pasture can swing a deal. He's going to expand his riding stable, and he needs another barn. Then

Sam had a good idea. He suggested selling the cottage and having it moved. The land around it is excellent. Moira and I might eventually move the garden business there."

"You'll lose money on the cottage."

"My first thought was burning it down. I think this will be better."

"You have a tendency to run to extremes, Alice. No, forget I said that. I understand. Though I never wanted Max killed. Or maybe just for a moment."

I thought that a moment was sometimes enough, but I didn't say it. I'd been there myself.

"There was no big moment of temptation and decision, you know," Herb continued. "It just slipped out. I mentioned that Max was getting carried away and that the manuscript could be awkward."

"That was enough with Bev in the picture."

"I didn't know about Bev. They kept that very quiet."

"And what about Forgette? Do you think he'll get off?"

"Yes, I do."

"It was murder."

"Vic was a multiple killer—apparently a real sociopath. Why he was employed for so long is anyone's guess."

"I have a few guesses," I said.

"Anyway, I'm told the evidence against him is very strong in Max's case. And Warren Landis's. They're looking at that hiker business as well. Besides, Forgette can claim self-defense. Vic was armed, he'd attacked you."

"And I say he was lying virtually helpless with a pitchfork in his arm."

Herb touched his sore shoulder. "Yeah. But by your own admission your blood alcohol count was through the roof, and you were under severe stress. A good defense attorney would go to town."

"He picked up the knife, you know. Had the police gotten there a few minutes later, he'd have killed me and been the hero—all witnesses dead. And how far he'd have been able to push poor dumb Salisbury is anyone's guess."

"Salisbury will be senator from Florida. Period."

"And Forgette will survive to run UB?"

"He'll have the best lawyers in the state."

"You included?"

"He won't have me—but he will get off. I hope you'll leave it at that, Alice."

"It's rough justice, I suppose. Though not for Bev and her family."

"But Max is in the clear."

"Max is over," I said, standing up. "Max is now out of the picture."

"I'm sorry."

"Me too. I'm sorry I hated him. I'm sorry I was so angry with him. Now I think, What was the point? After hate, you have regrets."

"I'm sorry about a lot of things," Herb said.

"But not about me. We're all square, Herb."

We shook hands, and he said, "Be happy, Alice."

Out the window, I saw Sam looking over the turquoise pool, the terraced yard, the emerald lawn. What sort of man was he? And what did he want? A house along these lines, God forbid? Some sort of vindication for failures personal and economic? Sam was still a stranger, an unknown territory where it behooved the explorer to tread carefully. But when he turned and caught my eye and smiled, I realized that I wasn't born for caution.

"I intend to try," I said.